SCENES FROM VILLAGE LIFE

Scenes from Village Life

Amos Oz

Translated from the Hebrew by
Nicholas de Lange

Chatto & Windus
LONDON

Published by Chatto & Windus 2011

2 4 6 8 10 9 7 5 3 1

Copyright © Amos Oz 2009
Translation copyright © Nicholas de Lange 2011

Amos Oz has asserted his right under the Copyright, Designs and Patents
Act 1988 to be identified as the author of this work

Nicholas de Lange has asserted his right under the Copyright, Designs and
Patents Act 1988 to be identified as the translator of this work

First published in Hebrew as *Tmunot Mihayei Hakfar* by
Keter Publishing House Ltd, POB 7145, Jerusalem, Israel

First published in Great Britain in 2011 by
Chatto & Windus
Random House, 20 Vauxhall Bridge Road,
London SW1V 2SA
www.randomhouse.co.uk

Addresses for companies within The Random House Group Limited
can be found at: www.randomhouse.co.uk/offices.htm

The Random House Group Limited Reg. No. 954009

A CIP catalogue record for this book
is available from the British Library

ISBN 9780701185503

The Random House Group Limited supports The Forest Stewardship Council®
(FSC®), the leading international forest certification organisation. All our titles
that are printed on Greenpeace approved FSC® certified paper carry the FSC®
logo. Our paper procurement policy can be found at:
www.randomhouse.co.uk/environment

Typeset in Sabon by Palimpsest Book Production Limited,
Falkirk, Stirlingshire

Printed and bound in Great Britain by
CPI Mackays Ltd, Chatham ME5 8TD

Contents

Heirs

1

THE STRANGER was not quite a stranger. Something in his appearance repelled and yet fascinated Arieh Zelnik from first glance, if it really was the first glance: he felt he remembered that face, the arms that came down nearly to the knees, but vaguely, as though from a lifetime ago.

The man parked his car right in front of the gate. It was a dusty, beige car, with a motley patchwork of stickers on the rear window and even on the side windows: a varied collection of declarations, warnings, slogans and exclamation marks. He locked the car, rattling each door vigorously to make sure they were all properly shut. Then he patted the bonnet lightly once or twice, as though the car were an old horse that you tethered to the gatepost and patted affectionately to let him know he wouldn't have long to wait. Then the man pushed the gate open and strode towards the vine-shaded front veranda.

He moved in a jerky, almost painful way, as if walking on hot sand.

From his swing seat in a corner of the veranda Arieh Zelnik could watch without being seen. He observed the uninvited guest from the moment he parked his car. But try as he might he could not remember where or when he had come across him before. Was it on a foreign trip? In the army? At work? At university? Or even at school? The man's face had a sly, jubilant expression, as if he had just pulled off a practical joke at someone else's expense. Somewhere behind or beneath the stranger's features there lurked the elusive suggestion of a familiar, disturbing face: was it someone who once harmed you, or someone to whom you yourself once did some forgotten wrong?

Like a dream of which nine-tenths had vanished and only the tail was still visible.

Arieh Zelnik decided not to get up to greet the newcomer but to wait for him here, on his swing seat on the front veranda.

As the stranger hurriedly bounced and wound his way along the path that led from the gate to the veranda steps, his little eyes darted this way and that as though he were afraid of being discovered too soon, or of being attacked by some ferocious dog that might suddenly leap out at him from the spiny bougainvillea bushes growing on either side of the path.

The thinning flaxen hair, the turkey-wattle neck, the watery, inquisitively darting eyes, the dangling chimpanzee arms, all evoked a certain vague unease.

From his concealed vantage point in the shade of a creeping vine, Arieh Zelnik noted that the man was large-framed but slightly flabby, as if he had just recovered from a serious illness, suggesting that he had been heavily built until quite recently, when he had begun to collapse inwards, and shrunk inside his skin. Even his grubby-beige summer jacket with its bulging pockets seemed too big for him, and hung loosely from his shoulders.

Though it was late summer and the path was dry, the stranger paused to wipe his feet carefully on the mat at the bottom of the steps, then inspected the sole of each shoe in turn. Only once he was satisfied did he go up the steps and try the mesh screen door at the top. After tapping on it politely several times without receiving any response he finally looked round and saw the householder planted calmly on his swing seat, surrounded by large flower pots and ferns in planters, in a corner of the veranda, in the shade of the arbour.

The visitor smiled broadly and seemed about to bow; he cleared his throat and declared:

'You've got a beautiful place here, Mr Zelkin! Stunning! It's a little bit of Provence in the State of Israel! Better than Provence – Tuscany! And the view! The woods! The vines! Tel Ilan is simply the loveliest village in this entire Levantine state. Very pretty! Good morning, Mr Zelkin. I hope I'm not disturbing you, by any chance?'

Arieh Zelnik returned the greeting drily, pointed out that his name was Zelnik, not Zelkin, and said that he was unfortunately not in the habit of buying anything from door-to-door salesmen.

'Quite right, too!' exclaimed the other, wiping his forehead with his sleeve. 'How can we tell if someone is a bona fide salesman or a con-man? Or even, heaven forbid, a criminal who is casing the joint for some gang of burglars? But as it happens, Mr Zelnik, I am not a salesman. I am Maftsir!'

'Who?'

'Maftsir. Wolff Maftsir. From the law firm Lotem & Pruzhinin. Pleased to meet you, Mr Zelnik. I have come, sir, on a matter, how should we put it, or perhaps instead of trying to describe it, we should come straight to the point. Do you mind if I sit down? It's a rather personal affair. Not my own personal affair, heaven forbid – if it were I would never dream of bursting in on you like this without prior notice. Although, in fact, we did try, we certainly did, we tried several times, but your telephone number is ex-directory and our letters went unanswered. Which is why we decided to try our luck with an unannounced visit, and we are very sorry for the intrusion. This is definitely not our usual practice, to intrude on the privacy of others, especially when they happen to reside in the most beautiful spot in the whole country. One way or another, as we have already remarked, this is on no account just our own personal business. No, no. By no means. In fact, quite the opposite: it concerns, how can we put it tactfully, it concerns your own personal affairs, sir. Your own personal affairs, not just ours. To be more precise, it relates to your family. Or perhaps rather to your family in a general sense, and more specifically to one particular member of your family. Would you object to us sitting and chatting for a few minutes? I promise you I'll do my best to ensure that the whole matter does not take up more than ten minutes of your time. Although, in fact, it's entirely up to you, Mr Zelkin.'

'Zelnik,' Arieh said.

And then he said: 'Sit down.'

'Not here, over there,' he added.

Because the fat man, or the formerly fat man, had first settled himself on the double swing seat, right next to his host, thigh to thigh. A cloud of thick smells clung to his body, smells of digestion, socks, talcum powder and armpits. A faint odour of pungent after-shave overlay the blend. Arieh Zelnik was suddenly reminded of his father, who had also covered his body odour with the pungent aroma of aftershave.

As soon as he was told to move, the visitor rose, swaying slightly, his simian arms holding his knees, apologised and deposited his posterior, garbed in trousers that were too big for him, at the indicated spot, on a wooden bench across the garden table. It was a rustic bench, made of roughly planed planks rather like railway sleepers. It was important to Arieh that his sick mother should not catch sight of this visitor, not even of his back, not even of his silhouette outlined against the arbour, which was why he had seated him in a place that was not visible from the window.

As for his unctuous, cantorial voice, her deafness would protect her from that.

2

IT WAS three years since Arieh Zelnik's wife, Na'ama, had gone off to visit her best friend Thelma Grant in San Diego and not come back. She had not written to say explicitly that she was leaving him, but had begun by hinting obliquely that she was not returning for a while. Six months later she had written: 'I'm still staying with Thelma.' And subsequently: 'No need to go on waiting for me. I'm working with Thelma in a rejuvenation studio.' And in another letter: 'Thelma and I get on well together, we have the same karma.' And another time: 'Our spiritual guide thinks that we shouldn't give each other up. You'll be fine. You're not angry, are you?'

Their married daughter, Hilla, wrote from Boston: 'Daddy, please, don't put pressure on Mummy. That's my advice. Get yourself a new life.'

And because he had long since lost contact with their elder child, their son Eldad, and he had no close friend outside the family, he had decided a year ago to get rid of his flat on Mount Carmel and move in with his mother in the old house in Tel Ilan, to live on the rent from two flats he owned in Haifa, and devote himself to his hobby.

So he had taken his daughter's advice and got himself a new life.

As a young man, Arieh Zelnik had served with the naval commandos. From his early childhood, he had feared no danger, no foe, no heights. But with the passage of the years he had come to dread the darkness of an empty house. That was why he had finally chosen to come back to live with his mother, in the old house where he had been born and raised, on the edge of this village, Tel Ilan. His mother, Rosalia, an old lady of ninety, was deaf, very bent, and taciturn. Most of the time, she let him take care of the household chores without making any demands or suggestions. Occasionally, the thought occurred to Arieh Zelnik that his mother might fall ill, or become so infirm that she could not manage without constant care, and that he would be forced to feed her, to wash her, and to change her nappies. He might have to employ a nurse, and then the calm of the household would be shattered and his life would be exposed to the gaze of outsiders. And sometimes, he even, or almost, looked forward to his mother's imminent decline, so that he would be rationally and emotionally justified in transferring her to a suitable institution and he would be left in sole occupancy of the house. He would be free to get a beautiful new wife. Or, instead of finding a wife, he could play host to a string of young girls. He could even knock down some internal walls and renovate the house. A new life would begin for him.

But in the meantime the two of them, mother and son, went on living together calmly and silently in the gloomy, old-fashioned house. A cleaner came every morning, bringing the shopping from a list he had given her. She tidied, cleaned and cooked, and after serving mother and son their midday meal she silently went on her way. The mother spent most of the day sitting in her room reading old books, while Arieh Zelnik listened to the radio in his own room or built model aircraft out of balsa wood.

3

SUDDENLY THE stranger flashed his host a sly, knowing smile that resembled a wink, as though suggesting that the two of them commit some small sin together, but fearing his suggestion might incur a punishment.

'Excuse me,' he asked in a friendly manner, 'would you mind if I helped myself to some of this?'

Thinking that his host had nodded consent, he poured some iced water with a slice of lemon and mint leaves from a jug into the only glass on the table, Arieh Zelnik's own glass, put his fleshy lips to it and swallowed the lot in five or six noisy gulps. He poured himself another half glass and thirstily downed that too.

'Sorry!' he said apologetically. 'Sitting on this beautiful veranda of yours, you simply don't realise how hot it is out there. It's really hot. But despite the heat this place is so charming! Tel Ilan really is the prettiest village in the whole country! Provence! Better than Provence – Tuscany! Woods! Vineyards! Hundred-year-old farmhouses, red roofs, and such tall cypresses! And now what do you think, sir? Would you prefer us to go on chatting about the beauty of the place, or will you permit me to move straight on to our little agenda?'

'I'm listening,' said Arieh Zelnik.

'The Zelniks, the descendants of Leon Akaviah Zelnik, were, if I am not mistaken, among the founders of this village. You were among the very first settlers, were you not? Ninety years ago? Nearly a hundred almost?'

'His name was Akiva Arieh, not Leon Akaviah.'

'Of course,' the visitor enthused. 'We have great respect for the history of your illustrious family. More than respect, admiration! First, if I am not mistaken, the two elder brothers, Semyon and Boris Zelkin, came from a little village in the district of Kharkov, to establish a brand-new settlement here in the heart of the wild landscape of the desolate Manasseh Hills. There was nothing here. Just a desolate plain covered in scrub. There were not even any Arab villages in this valley: they were all on the other side of the hills. Then their little nephew arrived, Leon, or, if you insist, Akaviah Arieh. And then, at least so the story goes, first Semyon and then Boris returned to Russia, where Boris killed Semyon with an axe, and only your grandfather – or was it your great-grandfather? – Leon Akaviah remained. What's that, he was called Akiva, not Akaviah? I'm sorry. Akiva then. To cut a long story short, it turns out that we, the Maftsirs, also come from Kharkov District! From the very forests of Kharkov! Maftsir! Maybe you've heard of us? We had a well-known cantor in the family, Shaya-Leib Maftsir, and there was also a certain Grigory Moiseyevich Maftsir, who was a very high-ranking general in the Red Army, until he was killed by Stalin, in the purges of the 1930s.'

The man stood up and mimed the stance of a member of a firing squad, making the sound of a salvo of rifle fire, and displaying sharp but not entirely white front teeth. He sat down again, smiling, on the bench, seemingly pleased with the success of the execution. Arieh Zelnik had the feeling the man might have been waiting for applause, or at least a smile, in exchange for his own saccharine grin.

The host chose, however, not to smile back. He pushed the used glass and the jug of iced water to one side, and said:

'Yes?'

Maftsir the lawyer clasped his left hand with his right hand and squeezed it joyfully, as if he had not met himself for a long time and this unexpected encounter filled him with gladness. Underneath the flood of words there bubbled up an inexhaustible gush of cheerfulness, a Gulf Stream of self-satisfaction.

'Well then. Let us begin to lay our cards on the table, as they say. The reason I took the liberty of intruding on you today has to do with the personal matters between us, and it may also have something to do with your dear mother, God grant her a long life. With that dear old lady, I mean to say. Always provided, of course, that you have no particular objection to broaching this delicate matter?'

'Yes,' said Arieh Zelnik.

The visitor stood up, took off his beige jacket, which was the colour of dirty sand, revealing large sweat marks under the armpits of his white shirt, hung the jacket on the back of his chair, and seated himself again.

'Excuse me,' he said. 'I hope you don't mind. It's just that it's such a hot day. Do you mind if I take my tie off too?' For a moment he looked like a frightened child, who knew that he deserved a reprimand but was too shy to beg. This expression soon vanished.

When his host said nothing, the man pulled his tie off, with a gesture that reminded Arieh Zelnik of his son Eldad.

'So long as we have your mother on our hands,' he remarked, 'we can't realise the value of the property, can we?'

'I beg your pardon?'

'Unless we find her an excellent place in a truly excellent home. And I happen to have such a home. Or rather, my partner's brother does. All we need is her consent. Or perhaps it would be simpler for us to certify that we have been appointed her guardians? In which case we would no longer require her consent.'

Arieh Zelnik nodded a few times and scratched the back of his right hand. It was true that once or twice recently he had found himself thinking about what would happen to his ailing mother, and to him, when she lost her physical or mental independence, and wondering when the moment to take a decision would come. There were moments when the possibility of parting from his mother filled him with sorrow and

16

shame, but there were also those moments when he almost looked forward to the possibilities that would open up before him when she was finally out of the house. Once he had even had Yossi Sasson, the estate agent, round to value the property. These suppressed hopes had filled him with feelings of guilt and self-loathing. He found it strange that this repulsive man seemed able to read his shameful thoughts. He therefore asked Mr Maftsir to go back to the beginning and explain precisely whom he represented. On whose behalf had he been sent here?

Wolff Maftsir chuckled:

'Not Mr Maftsir. Just call me Maftsir. Or Wolff. Between relatives there's no need for Mr.'

4

ARIEH ZELNIK stood up. He was a much taller and larger man than Wolff Maftsir and he had broader, stronger shoulders, even if they both had the same long arms that reached almost down to their knees. He took two steps towards his visitor and towered over him as he said:

'So what is it you want.'

He said these words without a question mark, and as he spoke he undid the top button of his shirt, revealing a glimpse of a grey, hairy chest.

'What's the hurry, sir,' Wolff Maftsir said in a conciliatory tone. 'Our business needs to be discussed carefully and patiently, from every angle, so as not to leave any chink or opening. We must not get our details wrong.'

To Arieh Zelnik the visitor looked limp or sagging. As though his skin were too big for him. Before he removed it, his jacket hung loosely from his shoulders, like an overcoat on a scarecrow. And his eyes were watery and rather murky. At the same time there was something scared about him, as though he feared a sudden insult.

'Our business?'

'I mean to say, the problem of the old lady. I mean your dear mother. Our property is still registered in her name and it will be until her dying day – and who can say what she has taken it into her head to write in her will – or until the two of us manage to get ourselves appointed her guardians.'

'The two of us?'

18

'This house could be knocked down and replaced by a sanatorium. A health farm. We could develop a place here that would be unequalled anywhere in the country: pure air, bucolic calm, rural scenery that's up there with Provence or Tuscany. Herbal treatments, massage, meditation, spiritual guidance, people would pay good money for what our place could offer them.'

'Excuse me, how long have we known each other exactly?'

'But we are old friends. More than that, we are relatives. Partners, even.'

By standing up Arieh Zelnik may have intended to make his visitor stand up too and take his leave. But the latter remained seated and even reached out to pour some more water with lemon and mint into the glass that had been Arieh Zelnik's until he had appropriated it. He leant back in his chair. Now, with the sweat marks in the armpits of his shirt, without his jacket and tie, Wolff Maftsir looked like a leisurely cattle dealer who had come to town to negotiate a deal, patiently and craftily, with the farmers, a deal from which, he was convinced, both sides would benefit. There was a hidden malicious glee in him, which was not entirely unfamiliar to his host.

'I have to go indoors now,' Arieh Zelnik lied. 'I have something to see to. Excuse me.'

'I'm in no hurry.' Wolff Maftsir smiled. 'If you have no objection I'll just sit and wait for you here. Or should I go inside with you and make the lady's acquaintance. After all, I haven't much time to gain her trust.'

'The lady,' Arieh Zelnik said, 'does not receive visitors.'

'I am not exactly a visitor,' Wolff Maftsir insisted, standing up ready to accompany his host indoors. 'After all, aren't we, so to speak, almost related? And even partners?'

Arieh Zelnik suddenly recalled his daughter Hilla's advice to give up her mother, not to strive to bring her back to him, and to try to start a new life. And surely the truth was that he had not fought very hard to bring Na'ama back: when she had gone off after a furious row to visit her best friend Thelma Grant, Arieh Zelnik had packed up all her clothes and belongings and sent them off to Thelma's address in San Diego. When his son Eldad severed all ties with him, he had packed up Eldad's books and even his childhood toys and sent them to him. He had cleared out every reminder of him, as one clears out an enemy position when the fighting is over. After a few more months, he had packed up his own belongings, given up the flat in Haifa, and moved in with his mother here in Tel Ilan. More than anything, he desired total peace and quiet: a succession of identical days and nothing but free time.

Sometimes he went for long walks round the village and beyond, among the hills that surrounded the little valley, through the fruit orchards and dusky pine woods. And sometimes he wandered for half an hour among the remains of his father's long-abandoned farm. There were still a few dilapidated buildings, chicken coops, corrugated-iron huts, a barn, the deserted shed where they had once fattened calves. The stables had become a storeroom for the furniture from his old flat on Mount Carmel, in Haifa. Here, in the former stables, the armchairs, sofa, rugs, sideboard, table gathered dust, all bound together with cobwebs. Even the old double bed he had shared with Na'ama was standing there on its side, in a corner. And the mattress was buried under piles of dusty quilts.

Arieh Zelnik said:

'Excuse me. I'm busy.'

Wolff Maftsir said:

'Of course. I'm sorry. I won't disturb you, my dear fellow. On the contrary. From now on I won't make a sound.'

He stood up and followed his host inside the house, which was dark and cool and smelt faintly of sweat and old age.

Arieh Zelnik said firmly:

'Please wait for me outside.'

Although what he had meant to say, even with a degree of rudeness, was that the visit was now over and that the stranger should push off.

5

BUT IT never even occurred to the visitor to leave. He floated indoors on Arieh Zelnik's heels and on the way, along the passageway, he opened each door in turn and calmly inspected the kitchen, the library, and the workroom where Arieh Zelnik pursued his hobby, and where model aircraft made of balsa wood hung from the ceiling, stirring slightly with each draught as though preparing for some ruthless aerial combat. He reminded Arieh Zelnik of the habit he himself had had, since childhood, of opening every closed door to see what lurked behind it.

When they reached the end of the passage Arieh Zelnik stood and blocked the entrance to his own bedroom, which had once been his father's. But Wolff Maftsir had no intention of invading his host's bedroom; instead he tapped gently on the deaf old lady's door, and as there was no reply he laid his hand caressingly on the handle and, opening the door gently, saw Rosalia lying on the big double bed, covered up to her chin with a blanket, her hair in a hairnet, eyes closed, and her angular, toothless jaw moving as if she were chewing.

'Just like in our dream,' Wolff Maftsir chuckled. 'Greetings, dear lady. We missed you so much and we were so longing to come to you, you must be very pleased to see us?'

So saying, he bent over and kissed her twice, a long kiss on either cheek, and then kissed her again on the forehead. The old lady opened her cloudy eyes, drew a skeletal hand out from under the

23

blanket and stroked Wolff Maftsir's head, murmuring something or other and pulling his head
towards her with both hands. In response, he bent
closer, took off his shoes, kissed her toothless mouth
and lay down at her side, pulling at the blanket to
cover them both.

'There,' he said. 'Hello, my very dear lady.'

Arieh Zelnik hesitated for a moment or two, and
looked out of the open window at a tumbledown
farm shed and a dusty cypress tree up which an
orange bougainvillea climbed with flaming fingers.
Walking round the double bed he closed the shutters and the window and drew the curtains, and as
he did so he unbuttoned his shirt, then undid his
belt, removed his shoes, undressed, and got into bed
next to his old mother, and so the three of them
lay, the woman whose house it was, her silent son,
and the stranger who kept stroking and kissing her
while he murmured softly, 'Everything is going to
be all right, dear lady. It's all going to be lovely.
We'll take care of everything.'

Relations

1

THE VILLAGE was swathed in the premature darkness of a February evening. Apart from Gili Steiner, there was no one else at the bus stop which was lit by a pale street lamp. The council offices were closed and shuttered. Sounds of television came through the shutters of the nearby houses. A stray cat padded on velvet paws past the rubbish bins, tail erect, belly slightly rounded. Slowly it crossed the road and vanished in the shade of the cypress trees.

The last bus from Tel Aviv reached Tel Ilan every evening at seven o'clock. Dr Gili Steiner had come to the bus stop in front of the council offices at twenty to seven. She worked as a family doctor at the Medical Fund clinic in the village. She was waiting for her nephew, Gideon Gat, her sister's son, who was in the army. He had been studying at the Armoured Corps training school when he was discovered to have a kidney problem that required hospitalisation. Now that he was out of hospital, his mother had sent him to convalesce for a few days with her sister in the country.

Dr Steiner was a thin, desiccated, angular-looking woman with short, grey hair, severe features and square rimless glasses. She was energetic yet looked older than her forty-five years. In Tel Ilan she was considered an excellent diagnostician – hardly ever wrong in her diagnosis – but people said she had a dry, abrasive manner and showed no sympathy for her patients: she was simply an attentive listener. She had never married, but people her age in the village remembered that when she was young she had had a love affair with a married man who was killed in the Lebanon War.

She sat on her own on the bench at the bus stop, waiting for her nephew and peering at her watch from time to time. In the faint glow of the street-light it was hard to make out the hands, and she could not tell how much time she had left to wait. She hoped the bus would not be late and that Gideon would be on board. He was an absent-minded young man, who was perfectly capable of getting on the wrong bus. Presumably, now that he was recovering from a serious illness, he was more absent-minded than ever.

Meanwhile, Dr Steiner inhaled the cool night air at the end of this cold, dry winter's day. Dogs were barking, and above the roof of the council offices hung an almost full moon that shed a skeletal, white light on the street, the cypresses and the hedges. The tops of the bare trees were wrapped in mist. In recent years Gili Steiner had joined a couple of classes run by Dalia Levin at the Village Hall but she had not found what she was looking for. What she was looking for she didn't really know. Perhaps her nephew's visit would help her to make some sense of things. For a few days the two of them would be alone together, sitting by the electric heater. She would look after him as she used to do when he was small. A conversation might start up, and she might be able to help this boy, whom she had loved all these years as though he were her own son, to recover his strength. She had filled the fridge with goodies and made his bed, and she had spread a woolly rug at the foot of the bed, in the room that had always been his, next to her own bedroom. On the bedside table she had placed some newspapers and magazines, and three or four books that she liked and that she hoped Gideon would like too. She had switched the boiler on so that there would be hot water for him, and had left a soft light and the heater on in the living room, and she had put out a bowl of fruit and some nuts, so he would feel at home as soon as they got in.

At ten past seven the rumble of the bus could be heard from the direction of Founders' Street. Dr Steiner stood up in front of the bus stop, wiry and determined, with a dark sweater over her angular shoulders and a dark woollen scarf round her neck. First, two older women alighted from the back door; Gili Steiner knew them slightly. She greeted them and they greeted her in return. Arieh Zelnik got off slowly, from the front door of the bus, wearing a military battledress that was a little too big for him and a cap that came down over his forehead and hid his eyes. He said good evening to Gili Steiner and asked her jokingly if she was waiting for him. No, she said, she was waiting for her nephew who was in the army, but Arieh Zelnik had not seen any soldier on the bus. Gili Steiner said she was referring to a soldier in civilian clothes. In the meantime, another three or four passengers had alighted but Gideon was not among them. The bus was almost empty now, and Gili asked Mirkin, the driver, if he hadn't noticed among the people who got on in Tel Aviv a tall, slim young man with glasses, a soldier on leave, quite good-looking but rather absent-minded and perhaps not in the best of health. Mirkin, the driver, could not recall anyone answering to that description, but said with a laugh:

'Don't you worry, Dr Steiner, whoever didn't arrive this evening will certainly turn up tomorrow morning, and whoever doesn't arrive tomorrow morning will come tomorrow lunchtime. Everyone gets here sooner or later.'

Gili Steiner asked the last passenger, Avraham Levin, as he got off, if there mightn't have been a young man on the bus who got off at the wrong stop by mistake.

'There may have been. And then again there may not have been,' said Avraham Levin. 'I wasn't paying attention. I was deep in thought.'

And after a moment's hesitation he added:

'There are a lot of stops along the way. And a lot of people got on and off.'

Mirkin, the driver, offered to drop Dr Steiner off on his way home. The bus spent every night parked outside Mirkin's house, and left for Tel Aviv at seven o'clock in the morning. Gili thanked him and said she preferred to walk home: she enjoyed the winter air, and now that it was clear her nephew hadn't come, she had no reason to hurry back.

After Mirkin had said goodnight and closed the door of the bus with a sigh of compressed air and was on his way home, Gili Steiner had second thoughts: it was quite possible that Gideon had fallen asleep lying on the back seat without anyone noticing, and now that Mirkin was parking the bus in front of his house, turning off the lights and locking the door, he would be a prisoner till the next morning. So she turned towards Founders' Street and strode energetically after the bus, with a view to cutting across the Memorial Garden that stood cloaked in darkness touched by the pale silver light of the moon.

2

WITHIN TWENTY or thirty paces Gili Steiner had made up her mind that, in fact, she should go straight home and ring Mirkin, the driver, to ask him to go outside and check if anyone had fallen asleep on the back seat of the bus. She could also ring her sister to find out whether Gideon had actually set off for Tel Ilan or if the trip had been cancelled at the last moment. On the other hand, what was the point of causing her sister unnecessary anxiety? It was enough that she herself was worried. If the boy had indeed got off at the wrong stop, he must be trying to ring her from one of the other villages. Another reason to go straight home and not run after the bus all the way to Mirkin's house. She would tell Gideon to take a taxi from wherever he was and, if he did not have enough money, she would of course pay the fare. She could see the boy in her mind's eye arriving at her home by taxi in another half-hour or so, smiling his usual shy smile, and apologising in his soft voice for getting muddled, and she would pay the taxi driver and hold Gideon's hand the way she used to when he was a child and calm him down and forgive him, and take him indoors to have a shower and to eat the supper she had prepared for them both, baked fish with baked potatoes. While he finished showering, she would take a quick look at his medical records, which she had asked Gideon to bring with him. When it came to diagnosis, she trusted only herself. And not necessarily even herself. Or not entirely.

Though she had made up her mind that she should definitely go straight home, Dr Steiner continued walking with small, firm steps up Founders' Street towards the Village Hall, turning off to take a short cut through the Memorial Garden. The damp winter air made her glasses mist up. She took them off, rubbed them hard with the end of her scarf, and thrust them back on her nose. For an instant, without the glasses, her face had looked less severe, taking on a gentle, offended look, like a little girl who had been scolded unfairly. But there was no one around in the Memorial Garden to see her. We all knew Dr Steiner only through the cold sheen of her square, rimless glasses.

The garden lay peaceful, silent and empty. Beyond the lawn and the bougainvillea bushes a clump of pines formed a dense, dark mass. Gili Steiner breathed deeply and quickened her pace. Her shoes grated on the gravel path as though they had picked up some tiny creature that was letting out truncated shrieks. When Gideon was four or five years old his mother had brought him to stay with his aunt, who had recently started working as a family doctor in Tel Ilan. He was a dozy, dreamy child, who could entertain himself for hours on end with a game that he played with three or four simple objects, a cup, an ashtray, a pair of shoelaces. Sometimes he would sit on the steps in front of the house, in his shorts and grubby shirt, staring into space, motionless except for his lips, which moved as if they were telling him a story. Aunt Gili was worried by his solitude and tried to find playmates for him, but the neighbours' children found him boring and after a quarter of an hour he would be on his own again. He made no attempt to make friends with them, but sprawled on the swing chair on the veranda, staring into space. Or lining up nails. She bought him some games and toys but the child did not play with them for long before returning to his regular pastime: two cups, an ashtray, a vase, a few paperclips and spoons that he arranged on the rug according to some logic that only he knew, then shuffled and rearranged them, his lips moving the whole time as though telling himself the stories that he never shared with his aunt. At night he fell asleep clutching a faded toy kangaroo.

Occasionally, she attempted to break through the child's solitude by suggesting a walk in the country-side, a visit to Victor Ezra's shop to buy sweets, or a climb up the water tower that stood on three concrete legs, but he simply shrugged his shoulders, as though surprised at her sudden and inexplicable access of activity.

On another occasion when Gideon was five or six, and his mother brought him to stay with his aunt, she had taken a few days off work. But when Gili was called out urgently to visit a patient on the outskirts of the village, the child insisted on staying in alone, to play on the rug with a toothbrush, a hairbrush and some empty matchboxes. She refused to let him stay at home alone, and insisted that he should either go with her or wait at the clinic under the supervision of the receptionist, Cilla. But he stood his ground: he wanted to stay at home. He was not afraid of being alone. His kangaroo would look after him. He promised not to open the door to strangers. Gili Steiner suddenly flew into a rage, not only at the child's stubborn insistence on staying on his own and playing his lonely games on the rug, but at his constant strangeness, his phlegmatic

manner, his kangaroo and his detachment from
the world. 'You're coming with me right now,' she
shouted, 'and that's that.' 'No, Aunt Gili, I'm
staying,' the child replied, gently and patiently, as
though surprised she was so slow on the uptake.
She raised her hand and slapped him hard on the
cheek, and then to her own amazement, she
continued to hit him with both hands, on his head,
his shoulders, his back, with fury, as though in a
fight with a bitter enemy or teaching a lesson to a
recalcitrant mule. Gideon curled up silently under
the hail of blows, with his head hunched between
his shoulders, waiting for the onslaught to end. Then
he looked up at her with wide eyes and asked her,
'Why do you hate me?' Startled, she hugged him
with tears in her eyes, kissed his head and allowed
him to stay at home on his own with his kangaroo,
and on her return, less than an hour later, she said
she was sorry. 'It's all right,' the child said, 'people
get angry sometimes.' But he redoubled his silence
and hardly spoke a word until his mother came to
collect him a couple of days later. Neither he nor
Gili told her about their quarrel. Before he left,
he picked up the rubber bands, the book-end, the

salt-shaker and the prescription pad from the rug and put them away. He put the kangaroo in its drawer. Gili leaned over and kissed him lovingly on both cheeks; he kissed her politely on her shoulder, with clenched lips.

3

S HE WALKED faster, feeling more certain with each step that Gideon had indeed fallen asleep on the back seat and was now locked in the dark bus parked for the night in front of Mirkin's house. She imagined him, woken by the cold and the sudden silence, trying to get out of the bus, pushing at the closed doors, thumping on the rear window. He had probably forgotten to bring his mobile phone, as usual, just as she had forgotten to take hers when she left home to go and wait for him at the bus stop.

A fine rain had begun to fall, and the breeze had dropped. Crossing the dark clump of pines, she reached the faint streetlamp at the Olive Street exit from the Memorial Garden. Here she tripped on an overturned dustbin. Carefully avoiding the bin, Gili

Steiner walked briskly up Olive Street. The shuttered houses were shrouded in a murky mist and
the well-kept gardens seemed to be sleeping in the
winter chill, surrounded by hedges of privet, myrtle
or thuja. Here and there a splendid new villa, built
on the ruins of an older house, leant out over the
street, covered in climbing plants. For some years
now wealthy city people had been buying up old
single-storey houses in Tel Ilan, razing them to the
ground, and replacing them with larger villas
adorned with cornices and awnings. Soon, Gili
Steiner thought to herself, Tel Ilan would stop being
a village and become a holiday resort for the wealthy.
She was going to leave her own home to her nephew
Gideon, and had already drawn up a will to that
effect. She could see Gideon clearly now, wrapped
in his warm overcoat, sleeping fitfully on the back
seat of the locked bus, parked in front of Mirkin's
house.

She shivered in the cold as she crossed the corner
of Synagogue Square. The drizzle had stopped now.
An empty plastic bag billowed in the breeze and
blew past her shoulder like a pale ghost. Walking
faster, Gili Steiner turned from Willow Street into

Cemetery Road, at the end of which Mirkin, the bus driver, lived across the road from the teacher Rachel Franco, and her old father Pesach Kedem. Once, when he was about twelve, Gideon had turned up alone at his aunt's house in Tel Ilan because he had quarrelled with his mother and decided to run away from home. His mother had locked him in his room because he had failed an exam, and he had taken some money from her handbag, escaped by the balcony, and come to Tel Ilan. He had a little bag with him, containing some socks and underwear and one or two clean shirts, and he asked Gili to take him in. She hugged the boy, made him some lunch, gave him the battered kangaroo he had played with when he was little, and then she rang his mother, even though relations between them were frosty. Gideon's mother came the next day and picked the child up without saying a single word to her sister, and Gideon gave in, sadly said goodbye to Gili and was dragged away in silence, his hand tightly clasped in that of his furious mother. And another time, some three years before this evening, when Gideon was about seventeen, he had come to stay with her to shut himself away in the peace and solitude of the village while preparing for his biology exams. She was supposed to help him prepare for the exams, but instead, like conspirators, they had played endless games of draughts, most of which she won. She never allowed him to beat her. After each defeat he said to her in his sleepy voice: 'Let's have just one more game.' They sat up late every evening watching films on the television, side by side on the sofa with a blanket over their knees. In the morning Gili Steiner went off to work at the clinic, leaving him some sliced bread, salad, cheese and a couple of hard-boiled eggs on the kitchen table. When she got home she found him asleep fully dressed on the sofa. He had tidied and cleaned the kitchen and neatly folded his bedclothes. After lunch they played draughts again, one game after another, almost without a word, instead of preparing for his exam. In the evening they watched a witty British comedy on television until nearly midnight, sitting shoulder to shoulder wrapped in the blue blanket even though the heater was on, both laughing for once. Next day the boy went home, and two days later he managed to pass his biology exam even though he had hardly revised. Gili Steiner lied to her sister on the phone, saying that he had revised for the exam, that she had helped him, and that he was wonderfully organised and hard-working. Gideon sent his aunt a book of poems by Yehuda Amichai and thanked her on the flyleaf for her help in preparing for the biology exam. She replied with a picture postcard showing the view of Tel Ilan from the top of the water tower. She thanked him for the book and added that if he felt like coming to stay with her again, for instance if he had any more exams, he shouldn't be shy to ask. His room was always there for him.

4

MIRKIN, THE bus driver, a widower in his sixties with a broad rear end, had changed into casual clothes, a baggy pair of tracksuit bottoms and a T-shirt advertising some company or other. He was surprised when Dr Steiner suddenly knocked on his door and asked if he would come outside and check with her whether there was a passenger asleep on the back seat of his bus.

Mirkin was a large, heavily built man; he was cheerful and chatty. His broad smile displayed big, uneven incisors and a tongue that protruded slightly over his lower lip. His guess was that Dr Steiner's nephew had probably got off the bus at some stop along the way by mistake and was now hitchhiking to Tel Ilan. In his view Dr Steiner should go home and wait for her nephew. Nevertheless, he agreed to get a torch and go with her to make sure that no passenger was trapped in the parked bus.

'He's not there, for sure, Dr Steiner, but if it'll make you happy let's go and check. Why not?'

'You don't happen to remember a tall, thin young man wearing glasses, a rather vague young man, but very polite?' she repeated.

'I had several young lads on board. I think there was one clown with a backpack and a guitar.'

'And none of them came all the way to Tel Ilan? They all got off on the way?'

'I'm sorry, Doctor. I don't remember. I don't suppose you've got some wonder drug to improve the memory? Recently I've been forgetting everything. Keys, names, dates, wallet, documents. If it goes on like this, I'll soon forget who I am.'

43

He opened the bus by pressing a hidden button under the step and climbed on board heavily, stirring jerkily dancing shadows with his torch as he searched each row of seats. Gili Steiner got on after him and nearly crashed into his broad back as he advanced down the aisle. When he reached the back row he let out a low exclamation of surprise as he bent down and picked up a shapeless bundle. He spread out an overcoat.

'That's not your visitor's coat is it, by any chance?'

'I'm not sure. Maybe.'

The driver flashed his torch on the coat, and then on the doctor's face, her short grey hair, her square glasses, her thin, stern lips, and suggested that the young man might have been on board the bus, got off at the wrong stop, and forgotten his overcoat.

Gili felt the coat with both hands, sniffed it, then asked the driver to flash his torch on it again.

'I think it's his. I'm not sure, though.'

'Take it,' the driver said magnanimously. 'Take it home with you. After all, if another passenger comes along tomorrow asking for it, I know where you live. Can I give you a lift home, Dr Steiner? It's going to start raining again soon.'

Gili thanked him and said there was no need, she would walk home, she had already bothered him more than enough in his time off. She got off the bus and the driver followed, lighting the steps for her with his torch. As she got off she put the coat on, and felt absolutely certain that it was Gideon's. She could remember it from the previous winter. A short, brown, shaggy coat. She enjoyed wearing it, and for an instant she had the impression that it held the young man's smell, not his smell now but when he was little, a faint smell of almond soap and porridge. The coat was only a little too big for her, and it was soft and pleasant to the touch.

She thanked Mirkin again, and he repeated his offer to drive her home, but she assured him there was really no need, and left. The almost full moon emerged once more from the clouds to shed its pale, silvery light on the tips of the cypresses in the nearby cemetery. A wide, deep silence descended on the village, broken only by the lowing of a cow some-where near the water tower, answered by distant dogs whose long, dim barking subsided into a howl.

5

B UT PERHAPS it wasn't Gideon's coat after all?
It was quite possible that he had cancelled his
trip and forgotten to let her know. Or maybe his
illness had got worse and he had been rushed back
to hospital? She knew from her sister that he had
contracted a kidney infection in the middle of one
of his courses at the Armoured Corps training
school, and had spent ten days in the nephrology
department of the hospital. Her sister had forbidden
her to visit him. The two sisters had been on bad
terms for a very long time. It was because she had
no information about the details of his illness, and
was very anxious, that she had asked him on the
phone to bring his medical records with him for her
to take a look at. When it came to a diagnosis, she
definitely did not trust any other doctor.

Or perhaps he wasn't ill, but had boarded the
wrong bus and fallen asleep, and woken up at the
final stop in the dark in some strange village and
was now wondering how on earth he would get
to Tel Ilan. She must hurry home. What if at this

very moment he was trying to phone her? Or
perhaps he had managed to make his own way
here and was sitting waiting for her on her front
steps? Once, when he was eight, his mother had
brought him here to stay during the winter holidays. She would bring him to stay with her sister
during the holidays, despite the long-standing rift
between them. The first night he had nightmares.
He groped his way in the dark to her room and
crawled into bed with her, trembling with fear, his
eyes wide open: there was a chuckling devil in his
room that was reaching out towards him with ten
long arms and black gloves on its hands. She
stroked his head and pressed him to her thin chest,
but the child refused to be comforted and kept on
making loud gasping sounds. So Gili Steiner
decided to get rid of the cause of his fear, and
forcibly dragged him, silent and paralysed with
terror, back to his bedroom. The child kicked and
struggled, but, undeterred, she held him firmly by
the shoulders and pushed and pulled him into the
room. Switching on the light, she showed him that
the source of his fear was merely a coat-stand with
some shirts and a sweater hanging from it. He did

not believe her and struggled to get free and, when he bit her, she slapped him twice, once on each cheek, to put an end to his hysterics. At once, regretting what she had done, she hugged him and pressed his cheek to hers, and then let him sleep in her bed with his battered kangaroo.

The next morning he seemed absorbed in his thoughts, but he did not ask to go home. Gili told him that he could sleep in her bed for the two nights that were left before his mother came to fetch him. Gideon made no mention of his nightmare. That night he insisted on sleeping in his own room, merely asking her to leave his door open and the light on in the passage. At two o'clock in the morning he crawled into her bed, trembling, and slept in her arms. She lay awake, breathing in the smell of the gentle shampoo she had washed his hair with the previous evening, knowing that a deep, wordless bond tied them to each other for ever, and that she loved this child more than she had loved any other being in the world and more than she would ever love anyone else.

6

THERE WAS not another living soul to be seen in the village, apart from the alley cats gathered around the dustbins. The anxious voice of the TV newsreader made its way through the shuttered windows. In the distance, a dog barked as if under orders to shatter the peace of the village. Gili Steiner, still wrapped in the overcoat Mirkin had given her, tripped hurriedly past Synagogue Square and along Olive Street, and unhesitatingly took the short cut across the darkened pinewood in the Memorial Garden. A night bird screeched out of the darkness, followed by the guttural croaking of frogs from the pond. She felt certain now that Gideon was sitting waiting for her in the dark on the steps in front of her locked front door. But then how could the coat she was now wearing have been left in Mirkin's bus? Perhaps she was wearing a stranger's coat, after all? She began walking even faster. Gideon must be sitting there wearing his own coat, wondering what had happened to her. As she came out of the little wood, she was startled to see a figure sitting bolt upright, motionless, collar turned up, on a bench in the garden. After a moment's hesitation she boldly decided to get closer to have a look. It was merely a fallen branch, lying slantwise across the bench.

By the time Gili Steiner got home it was close to nine o'clock. She switched on the light in the entrance hall, turned off the water heater, and hurried to check for messages on the phone and also on her mobile, which she had forgotten on the kitchen table. No messages, though somebody had rung and hung up. Gili rang Gideon's mobile, but a recorded voice told her that the person she was calling was not available. She therefore made up her mind to swallow her pride and phone her sister in Tel Aviv to find out if Gideon had actually left or if he had decided to cancel the trip without telling her. The phone rang repeatedly, but there was no reply apart from the answering machine inviting her to leave a message after the beep. After a moment's hesitation she decided not to leave a message, because she could not think of anything to say: if Gideon had got lost and was on his way now, having hitched a lift or taken a taxi, there was no point in alarming his mother. And if he had decided to stay at home, he would surely have told her. Or he might have thought it wasn't important enough to ring her about tonight, in which case he would ring her at work tomorrow morning. But maybe his condition had deteriorated and he had had to go back to hospital? Maybe his temperature had shot up, the infection had recurred? At once she made up her mind to ignore her sister's veto and go to visit him in hospital after work tomorrow. She would go to the staff room and have a word with the head of department. She would ask to be allowed to look at the results of his tests and form her own opinion.

Gili took off the overcoat and examined it closely under the kitchen light. The colour was about right, but the collar seemed slightly different. She spread the coat out on the table, sat down on one of the two kitchen chairs and examined it carefully. The meal she had prepared for them, baked fish with baked potatoes, was ready to be reheated in the oven. She decided to wait for Gideon, and in the meantime switched on a little electric heater whose coils made soft popping sounds as they warmed up. She sat motionless for a quarter of an hour. Then she stood up and went to Gideon's room. The bed was made, at its foot was the warm rug, and on the bedside table were the newspapers, magazines and books that she had carefully chosen for him. Gili lit the little bedside lamp and plumped up the pillows. For an instant she had the feeling that Gideon had already been there, that he had slept the night, got up, made his bed and left, and she was once more on her own. Just as she remained alone in her empty house after each of his visits.

She bent over to tuck the bottom corners of the blanket under the mattress. Going back to the kitchen she sliced some bread, took the butter and cheese out of the refrigerator and put the kettle on. When the water boiled, she turned on the little radio that stood on the kitchen table. Three voices were arguing about the continuing crisis in agriculture, interrupting each other rudely. She turned it off and looked out of the window. Her front path was faintly lit and above the empty street the moon floated among broken low clouds. He's got a girlfriend, she suddenly thought, that's it, that's why he forgot to come and forgot to let me know: he's found himself a girl at last, so he has no reason to come and see me any more. The thought filled her with near unbearable pain. As though she had been completely emptied and only her shrivelled husk continued to hurt. He hadn't actually promised to come, he had just said that he would try to catch the evening bus, and she mustn't wait for him at the stop, because if he did decide to come tonight he would make his own way to her house, and if he didn't come tonight, he'd come some time soon, maybe next week.

Nevertheless, Gili Steiner could not shake off the thought that Gideon had lost his way, that he had got on the wrong bus, or got off at the wrong stop, and was now probably stuck on his own in some godforsaken spot, shivering with cold at a deserted bus stop, huddled on a metal bench behind an iron railing, between a closed ticket office and a locked news-stand. And he didn't know how to reach her. It was her duty to get up and go, now, this very minute, into the darkness, to search for him and find him and bring him safely home.

Around ten o'clock Gili Steiner said to herself that Gideon would not come this evening and that there was really nothing for her to do except to warm up the fish and potatoes in the oven and eat them on her own, then go to bed and get up tomorrow before seven and go to the clinic to look after her irritating patients. She stood up, bent over, took the fish and potatoes out of the oven and threw them in the bin. Then she switched off the electric heater, sat down in the kitchen, took off her square, frameless glasses and cried, but after a minute or two she stopped, buried the battered kangaroo in the drawer, took the laundry out of the dryer, and until almost midnight she ironed and folded everything and put it away. At midnight she undressed and got into bed. It had begun to rain in Tel Ilan, and it rained on and off all night.

Digging

1

A s the end of his life approached, Pesach Kedem, the former Member of the Knesset, lived with his daughter Rachel, on the edge of the village of Tel Ilan in the Menasseh Hills. He was a tall, vituperative man with a hunched back. On account of kyphosis his head was thrust forward almost at a right angle. At eighty-six years of age, he was gnarled and sinewy, his skin reminded you of the bark of an olive tree, and his tempestuous temperament made him seem to be boiling over with strongly held ideals and opinions. All day long he pottered around the house in his slippers, wearing a singlet and a pair of khaki trousers that were too loose on him and were held up by braces. He invariably wore a shabby black beret that came halfway down his forehead, which made him look like a tank commander put out to grass. And he never stopped grumbling: he swore at a drawer that refused to open, cursed the newsreader who muddled Slovakia and Slovenia, railed at the westerly wind that got up suddenly and scattered his papers on the veranda table, and shouted at himself because when he bent down to pick them up he bumped into the corner of the table as he stood up.

He had never forgiven his Party for falling apart and disappearing twenty-five years earlier. He was pitiless in his criticism of his opponents and enemies, all of them long since deceased. The younger generation, electronics and modern literature all earned his disgust. The newspapers published nothing but filth. Even the man who presented the weather forecast on the television seemed to him like an arrogant matinee idol who mumbled nonsense and had no idea what he was talking about.

He deliberately confused or 'forgot' the names of present-day political leaders, just as the world had forgotten him. He, however, had forgotten nothing: he remembered the tiniest details of every insult, resented every wrong that had been done to him two and a half generations earlier, kept a mental note of every weakness shown by his opponents, every opportunistic vote in the Knesset, every glib lie ever uttered in committee, every disgrace brought on themselves by his comrades of forty years ago (whom he tended to refer to as false comrades, and, in the case of two junior ministers of his day, Comrade Hopeless and Comrade Useless).

One evening, as he was sitting with his daughter Rachel at the veranda table, he suddenly waved a pot of hot tea in the air and roared:

'A fine figure they cut, the whole lot of 'em, when Ben Gurion took off for London to flirt with Jabotinsky behind their backs!'

'Pesach,' his daughter said, 'put that teapot down, if you don't mind. Yesterday you splashed me with yoghurt and any minute now you're going to scald both of us.'

The old man even bore a grudge against his beloved daughter. True, she looked after him irreproachably every day, but she showed him no respect. Every morning she banished him from his bed at seven-thirty so that she could air or change the sheets, because he always smelt like over-ripe cheese. She never hesitated to comment on his body odour, and in the summer she would make him shower twice a day. Twice a week she would wash and brush his hair and launder his black beret. She was always throwing him out of the kitchen, because he would rummage in the drawers, searching for the chocolate that she hid from him: she never allowed him more than a square or two a day. Reproachfully she would remind him to flush the lavatory and pull up the zip of his flies. Three times a day she laid out a long line of little bottles containing the pills and capsules he had to take. All this Rachel did firmly, with economical, angular movements and pursed lips, as though it were her job to re-educate her ageing father, to correct his bad habits and finally wean him off a long life of selfishness and self-indulgence.

To cap it all, the old man had begun to complain in the morning of workmen who were digging under the house in the night and disturbing his sleep, as though they couldn't dig in the daytime, when decent law-abiding people were not asleep.

'Digging? Who's digging?'

'That's what I'm asking you, Rachel, who is it that's digging here at night?'

'Nobody's digging, during the day or at night, except perhaps in your dreams.'

'They *are* digging, I tell you! It starts an hour or two after midnight, all sorts of tapping and scraping sounds. You must be sleeping the sleep of the just if you don't hear it. You always were a heavy sleeper. What are they digging for, in the cellar or under the foundations? Oil? Gold? Buried treasure?'

Rachel changed the old man's sleeping pills, but it was no good. He went on complaining of knocking and digging sounds right under the floor of his bedroom.

2

RACHEL FRANCO, a good-looking, well-groomed widow in her mid-forties, taught literature in the village school. She was always tastefully dressed in full skirts in attractive pastel colours, with a matching scarf, delicate earrings and occasionally a silver necklace, and she wore high-heeled shoes even for work. Some people in the village looked askance at her girlish figure and her ponytail. (A woman of her age! And her a teacher, too! And a widow! Who is she titivating herself like that for? Micky the vet?

Her little Arab perhaps? Who is she trying to impress?)

The village was old and sleepy, a hundred years old or more, with leafy trees and red roofs, and agricultural smallholdings, many of which had been transformed into shops selling wines from boutique wineries, spicy olives, farmhouse cheeses, exotic flavourings and rare fruits, or macramé. The former farm buildings had been transformed into small galleries showing imported art works, decorative toys from Africa or items of furniture from India, which were sold to the visitors who streamed in from the towns in convoys every weekend, on the lookout for that original, exquisite find.

Rachel and her father lived in the secluded little house on the edge of the village, whose large garden abutted on the cypress hedge of the local cemetery. Both of them had been widowed. Abigail, the wife of Pesach Kedem MK, had died of blood poisoning many years previously. Their elder son, Eliaz, had died accidentally (he was the first Israeli to drown in the Red Sea, in 1949). As for Rachel's husband, Danny Franco, he had died of cardiac arrest on his fiftieth birthday.

Danny and Rachel Franco's younger daughter, Yifat, was married to a prosperous dentist in Los Angeles. Yifat's older sister, Osnat, was a diamond dealer in Brussels. Both daughters had distanced themselves from their mother, as though they held her responsible for their father's death, and they both disliked their grandfather, whom they considered spoilt, selfish and cantankerous.

Sometimes the old man, in a fit of rage, would call Rachel by her mother's name:

'No, seriously, Abigail, that was really beneath you. Shame on you!'

More rarely, when he was ill, he confused Rachel with his own mother, Hinde, who had been killed by Germans in a small village near Riga. When Rachel corrected him, he would angrily deny that he had made the mistake.

Rachel, however, never made a mistake where her father was concerned. She bore his apocalyptic rantings and reproofs stoically, but she reacted ruthlessly to every display of sloppiness or self-indulgence. If he forgot to lift the seat when he went to the toilet she would thrust a damp cloth in his hand and unceremoniously send him back to do what any civilised person should do. If he spilt soup on his trousers, she made him get up from the table at once and go to his room and change. She would not let him get away with buttoning up his shirt wrongly or walking about with his trouser leg caught in his sock. Whenever she told him off, for sitting in the toilet for forty-five minutes, or forgetting to lock the door, she called him by his name, Pesach. If she was exceptionally angry, she would address him as Comrade Kedem. But sometimes, very rarely, his loneliness or sadness stirred a fleeting pang of motherly tenderness in her. If, for instance, he turned up at the kitchen door with a hangdog air and pleaded like a child for another piece of chocolate, she might grant his request and even call him Daddy.

'They're boring underneath the house again. In the early hours of the morning I heard the sound of picks and shovels. Didn't you hear anything?'

'No, and you didn't either. You were imagining it.'

'What are they looking for underneath the house, Rachel? Who are these workmen?'

'Maybe they're digging a tunnel for the underground railway.'

'You're just making fun of me. But I'm not

imagining things, Rachel. There is someone digging under the house. Tonight I'll wake you up, so that you can hear it too.'

'There's nothing to hear, Pesach. There's no one burrowing down there, except perhaps your bad conscience.'

3

THE OLD man spent most of the day sprawled on a deckchair on the paved area in front of the house. If he felt restless he would get up and flit like an evil spirit from room to room, go down to the cellar to set traps for the mice, wrestle with the screen door to the veranda, pulling at it furiously even though it opened outwards, or curse his daughter's cats, that fled at the sound of his slippered feet. He would go down into the old farmyard, his head thrust forward almost at a right angle which gave him the look of an inverted hoe, frantically searching for some pamphlet or letter in the abandoned incubator, the fertiliser store, the toolshed, then forgetting what he had come for, picking up a discarded hoe with both hands, and starting to dig out an unnecessary channel between two beds, cursing himself for his own stupidity, cursing the Arab student who hadn't cleared the piles of dead leaves, dropping the hoe and re-entering the house by the kitchen door. In the kitchen he opened the door of the refrigerator, peered inside at the pallid light, slammed the door shut with a force that rattled the bottles, furiously crossed the corridor, muttering something to himself, perhaps denouncing the dead Socialist icons Yitzhak Tabenkin and Meir Ya'ari, looked into the bathroom, cursing the Socialist International, marched into his bedroom, then drawn irresistibly back into the kitchen, his beret-clad head thrust forward like a charging bull, searched in the larder and the cupboards for a piece of chocolate, groaning, slamming the cupboard doors, his white moustache bristling, staring out of the kitchen window and suddenly shaking a bony fist at a stray goat near the hedge or at an olive tree on the hillside, then once more padding with amazing agility from room to room, from cupboard to cupboard, where he had to find some vital document, immediately, urgently, his little grey eyes darting hither and thither, exploring every shelf or bookcase, all the time expounding his complaints to an invisible audience, with long strings of arguments, objections, insults and rebuttals. He was firmly resolved tonight to get out of bed and make his way down to the cellar with a bright torch to catch those diggers, whoever they might be.

4

EVER SINCE Danny Franco died and Osnat and Yifat left home and went abroad, father and daughter had no close relatives or friends. Their neighbours rarely sought their company and they hardly ever visited the neighbours. Pesach Kedem's contemporaries had passed away or were fading, but even before he had not had friends or disciples. It was Tabenkin himself who had gradually ousted him from the inner circle of the Party leadership. Rachel's school work stayed at school. The boy from Victor Ezra's grocery delivered whatever Rachel ordered by phone, and carried it into the house by the kitchen door. Strangers only rarely crossed the threshold of the last house, by the cypress hedge of the cemetery. Occasionally someone from the Village Council came and asked Rachel to prune her hedge that was getting overgrown and blocking the road, or a travelling salesman came to offer them a dishwasher or tumble dryer on easy repayment terms. (The old man exploded: an electric dryer?! What's that for? Has the sun retired? Have the washing lines all converted to Islam?) Once in a while a neighbour, a tight-lipped farm worker in blue overalls, knocked on the door to ask if they hadn't seen his lost dog in their garden. (A dog?! In our garden?! Rachel's cats would tear it to pieces!)

Ever since the student had taken up residence in the little building that had once served Danny Franco as his tool shed and housed the incubator for his chicks, the villagers sometimes paused near the hedge as though sniffing the air, then hurried on their way.

Sometimes Rachel, the literature teacher, and her father, the former MK, were invited to the home of one of the other teachers for a drink to celebrate the end of the school year, or to come and listen to a visiting speaker addressing a group at the house of one of the veteran residents of the village. Rachel would accept the invitation with thanks, but it usually turned out that a few hours before the party or the meeting the old man had an attack of emphysema or mislaid his dentures, so Rachel would ring and offer apologies on behalf of both of them. Occasionally Rachel would go on her own to a communal singing evening at the home of Dalia and Avraham Levin, a pair of teachers who had lost their child, and who lived further up the hill.

The old man particularly detested the three or four teachers from outside the village, who lived in rented rooms and returned to their families in the city at weekends. To relieve their loneliness, one or other of them would sometimes pop in to see Rachel, to borrow or return a book, to ask her advice on some question of teaching or discipline, or to woo her furtively. Pesach Kedem loathed these uninvited guests: he firmly believed that he and his daughter were enough company for each other, and they had no desire for unnecessary visits from strangers, whose motives were dubious and the devil only knew what they were really after. He was of the opinion that these days everybody's intentions were self-centred, not to say shady. The time was long past when some people at least could like or love one another without making all kinds of calculations. Nowadays, he repeatedly preached to his daughter, everyone, without exception, had ulterior motives, they were only interested in seeing how they could garner a few crumbs from someone else's table. A long life full of disillusionment had taught him that no one knocked at your door except in the hope of deriving some profit, advantage or benefit. Everything was calculated these days, and the calculations were generally disreputable. I tell you, Abigail, as far as I'm concerned they can all do us a favour and stay in their own homes. What do they think this is – the town square? A public saloon? A schoolroom? And while we're on the subject, just answer me this: what do we need with that Arab of yours?

Rachel corrected him:

'I'm not Abigail, I'm Rachel.'

The old man shut up at once, ashamed of his mistake and perhaps also regretting some of the things he had said. But after five or ten minutes he would start wheedling, like a child tugging at her sleeve:

'Rachel, I've got a pain.'

'Where?'

'In my neck. Or my head. My shoulders. No, not there, slightly lower down. Yes, there. You have a wonderful touch, Rachel.'

And then he would add shyly:

'I do love you, child. Really. I love you lots and lots.'

And a moment later:

'I'm very sorry I worried you. We won't let the digging in the night frighten us. Next time I'll go down to the cellar with an iron bar, come what may. I won't wake you. I've bothered you enough already. Even in the old days there were some comrades who called me a nuisance behind my back. Only about your Arab, I just want to say –'

'Shut up, Pesach.'

The old man would blink and do as she said, his white moustache quivering. And so the two of them sat at the veranda table in the evening breeze, she in jeans and a short-sleeved blouse, he in his baggy khaki trousers held up by braces, a hunchbacked man in a shabby, black beret, with a fine, slightly aquiline nose, and with sunken lips, but with white, youthful, perfect false teeth, which on the rare occasions when he smiled gleamed like those of a fashion model. His moustache, when it was not bristling with rage, looked white and fluffy, as though it were made of cotton wool. But if the newsreader on the radio irritated him, he would thump angrily on the table with his bony fist and declare:

'What an imbecile that woman is!'

5

O
N THE rare occasions when Rachel had visitors – colleagues from school, workmen, Benny Avni the Mayor, or Micky the vet – the old man flew into a rage like a swarm of bees, his thin lips tightened into the expression of an elderly inquisitor, and he would flee the sitting room and hole up in his regular lookout post, behind the partly-opened kitchen door. Here, barely suppressing a sigh, he would sit down on a green-painted stool and wait for the visitor to disappear. Meanwhile, he would strain to hear what was said between Rachel and the vet, say, thrusting his wrinkled neck

forward like a tortoise trying to reach a lettuce leaf, extending his head at an angle so as to get his good ear closer to the crack in the door.

'Where on earth did you get an idea like that from?' Rachel asked the vet.

'Well, you started it.'

Rachel's laugh tinkled lightly, like clinking glasses.

'Micky, honestly. Don't play with words. You know very well what I mean.'

'You're even more wonderful when you're angry.'

The old man, from his hiding place, wished them both an attack of foot and mouth disease.

'Look at this kitten, Micky,' Rachel said. 'He's barely three weeks old, sometimes he can hardly put one foot in front of the other, he tries to go down the steps and ends up rolling down like a little ball of wool, and then he makes such an endearing face, like a tiny suffering saint, but he has already learnt how to hide behind a cushion and peer out at me like a tiger in the jungle, his little body flattened and swaying from side to side, ready to pounce, and then he pounces, but he misjudges the distance and does a belly flop on the floor. In a year's time no female cat in the village will be able to resist his charms.'

'I'll have neutered him before then,' answered the vet. 'Before he can charm you, too.'

'I'll do the same to you,' murmurs the old man from behind the kitchen door.

Rachel pours the vet a glass of cold water and offers him some fruit and biscuits, while he is still joking with her in his easy-going way. Then she helps him to catch three or four cats that have to have their shots. He puts one cat in a cage: he'll take her away with him and bring her back with her wound dressed and sterilised, and in a couple of days she'll be as good as new. On one condition: that Rachel speaks at least one kind word to him. Kind words matter more to him than money.

'What a scoundrel!' whispers the old man in his hiding place. 'A wolf in vet's clothing.'

Micky the vet has a little Peugeot truck, which the old man insists on calling a Fiji, like the islands. His greasy hair is tied up in a ponytail, and he wears an earring in his right ear. Both these make the former MK's blood boil: 'If I've warned you once against that villain, I've warned you a thousand times –'

Rachel, as always, cuts him short:

'That's enough, Pesach. After all, he's a member of your Party.'

These words rouse the old man to a renewed outburst of rage:

'My Party? My Party died years ago, Abigail! First they prostituted my Party and then they buried it ignominiously! As it deserved!'

Then he launched into a tirade against his dead comrades, his false comrades, his comrades in double inverted commas, Comrade Hopeless and Comrade Useless, those two traitors who became his enemies and persecutors just because he clung to the bitter end to the principles that they sold for a mess of pottage on every high hill and under every green tree. All that was left of those false friends now, and of the entire Party, was just worminess and decay. The last phrase was borrowed from Bialik, although he had a grudge against Bialik: in the evening of his days Bialik had turned from being the national prophet of rage into a sort of provincial gentleman, who accepted the post of Commissar for Culture, if not worse, under Meir Dizengoff.

'But let's get back to your disgusting hooligan.

That fattened calf! A calf with a ring in his ear! A gold ring in a pig's nose! That braggart! That windbag! That prattler! Even your little Arab student is a hundred times more cultured than that beast!'

'Pesach,' said Rachel.

The old man shut up, but his heart was bursting with loathing for *that* Micky – with his big behind and his T-shirt with 'Come on baby, let's have fun!' written on it in English – and with sorrow for these terrible times, when there was no more room for affection between people, for forgiveness or compassion.

Micky the vet visited the house by the cemetery two or three times a year, to see to the new generation of cats. He was one of those people who like to speak of themselves in the third person, and using their nickname. 'So I said to myself, it's time for Micky to take himself in hand. Otherwise it simply won't work.' A broken incisor gave him the look of a dangerous brawler. His walk was lazy but springy, like that of a drowsy beast of prey. In his murky grey eyes there sometimes flashed a spark of suppressed licentiousness. While he was talking he occasionally reached behind him to ease the seat of his trousers that had got caught in the cleft of his buttocks.

76

'Shall I vaccinate that Arab student who lives in your kennel, too?' the vet suggested.

Despite this offer, he stayed on for a while with the student when he had finished his work, and even beat him at draughts.

All kinds of rumours buzzed round the village about the Arab boy who lived at Rachel Franco's, and Micky the vet hoped to take advantage of the opportunity and the game of draughts to sniff out any hint of what was really going on. And even though he did not discover anything, he was able to tell people in the village that the Arab was twenty or twenty-five years younger than Rachel, easily young enough to be her son, and that he lived in a shed in the back garden which she had fitted out with a desk and a bookcase – so he was an intellectual. The vet could also report that Rachel and the boy were, how to put it, not exactly indifferent to each other. No, he hadn't caught them holding hands or anything like that, but he had seen the boy hanging out her washing on the line behind the house. Even her underwear.

6

WEARING A singlet and baggy underpants the old man stood in the bathroom with his legs spread wide apart. He had forgotten to lock the door again. Again he had forgotten to lift the seat before using the toilet. Now he was leaning over the basin, frenziedly scrubbing his face, his shoulders, his neck, splashing water in every direction like a wet dog, snorting and gurgling under the jet of water, squeezing his left nostril so as to empty the contents of the right nostril into the basin, then pressing the right one so as to empty the other, clearing his throat, expectorating four or five times until the sputum was freed from his chest and projected against the side of the basin, and finally pummelling himself dry with a thick towel, as though he were scouring a frying pan.

When he was dry he put on a shirt, buttoning it up wrongly, and his shabby black beret, and stood hesitantly in the corridor for a while, his head thrust forward almost at a right angle, silently chewing his tongue. Then he wandered from room to room and went down into the cellar, looking for telltale signs of the nocturnal digging, cursing the workmen who had managed to erase every trace of their activity, unless perhaps it was deeper, under the floor of the cellar, in the foundations, under the heavy earth. From the cellar he went up to the kitchen, and out through the kitchen door into the yard, among the abandoned sheds, striding angrily to the far end. On his return he found Rachel sitting at the table on the veranda, bent over some marking. From the steps he said to her:

'But on the other hand, I am pretty repulsive myself. As you must admit. So what do you need with that vet of yours? Isn't one repulsive man enough for you?'

Then he added sadly, referring to Rachel in the third person, as though she were not present:

'I need a piece of chocolate every now and then, to bring some sweetness into my dark life, but she hides it from me as though I were a burglar. She doesn't understand anything. She thinks I need the chocolate because I'm greedy. Wrong! I need it because my body has stopped producing sweetness of its own. I haven't got enough sugar in my blood and my tissues. She understands nothing! She's so cruel! So cruel!'

And on reaching the door of his bedroom he stopped, turned and shouted to her:

'And all these cats only bring diseases! Fleas! Germs!'

7

THE ARAB student was the son of an old friend of Danny Franco, Rachel's husband who went and died on his fiftieth birthday. What was the nature of the friendship between Danny Franco and Adel's father? Rachel didn't know, and Adel didn't talk about it. Maybe he didn't know either.

He had appeared one morning the previous summer, introduced himself, and asked shyly if he could rent a room. Well, not exactly rent. And not exactly a room. A couple of years ago, Danny of blessed memory, what a wonderful man he was, had offered Adel's father to put his son up in one of the farm outbuildings, because the farm was no longer a working one and the sheds and outhouses were all standing empty. He had come now to enquire if the offer made two years ago was still valid. That is, if there was still a shed free for him right now. In return he was willing, for example, to weed the yard or help with household chores. It was like this: he had taken a year off his course at university, and was planning to write a book. Yes, something about life in a Jewish village compared to life in an Arab village, a scholarly study or a novel, he hadn't decided yet for sure, and so he needed – it would suit him well – to live on his own for a while on the edge of Tel Ilan. He remembered the village, with all its vineyards and fruit orchards and the view of the Menasseh Hills, from a single visit he had paid with his father and his sisters when he was a child, to Danny of blessed memory. Danny of blessed memory had invited them to come and spend a whole day here, maybe Rachel could still remember that visit? No? Of course she didn't, there was no particular reason why she should. But he, Adel, had not forgotten it and never would. He had always hoped some day to return to the village of Tel Ilan. To return to this house next to the tall cypresses of the cemetery. 'It's so peaceful here, much more peaceful than our village, which has grown so much it isn't a village any more, it's a small town now, full of shops and garages and dusty car parks.' It was because it was so beautiful that he had dreamed of returning. And because of the peace and quiet. And because of something else that he couldn't define but that he might succeed in describing in the book he wanted to write. He would write about the differences between a Jewish village and an Arab village. 'Your village was born out of a dream and a plan, and our village was not born, it's always been there, but still they do have something in common. We have dreams, too. No, comparisons are always false. But the thing that I love here, that isn't false. I can pickle cucumbers, too, and make jam. Only if there's a need for such things here, of course. And I have some experience of painting, and even mending roofs. And keeping bees, too, if by any chance you feel like renewing your days as of old, as you Jews say, and having a few beehives. I won't make any noise or leave any mess. And in my spare time I'll prepare for my exams and start writing my book.'

8

ADEL WALKED with a stoop. He was a shy yet talkative young man, and wore glasses that were too small for him, as though he had taken them from some child, or had kept them from his own childhood. They were secured by a string, and had a tendency to mist up, so that he had to keep wiping them with the tail of the shirt that he always wore outside his threadbare jeans. He had a dimple in his left cheek that also gave him a shy, childlike look. He shaved only his chin and sideburns; the rest of his face was smooth and hairless. His shoes looked too big and too coarse for him, and they left strange, menacing footprints on the dusty courtyard. When he watered the fruit trees they made puddles in the mud. He bit his fingernails, and his hands were red and rough as if from the cold. He was fine-featured, apart from his thick lower lip. When he smoked he sucked so hard on the cigarette that his cheeks caved in and for a moment the outline of his skull seemed to be revealed beneath his skin.

Adel walked around the yard wearing a Van Gogh straw hat and an expression of wonderment and longing. His shoulders were always covered with a powdering of dandruff. He had an absent-minded way of smoking: he would light a cigarette, draw on it three or four times, sucking his cheeks right in, then put it down on the fence or the windowsill, forget the lit cigarette and light another one. A reserve cigarette was always tucked behind his ear. He smoked a lot, but always with an air of disgust, as if he hated the smoke and the smell of tobacco, as if it were someone else who was smoking and puffing the smoke in his face. He also developed a special relationship with Rachel's cats: he had long, respectful conversations with them, always in Arabic, and in a low voice as though letting them into a secret.

Former MK Pesach Kedem did not like the student. 'You can see right away,' the old man said, 'that he hates us but hides his hatred under a layer of sycophancy. They all hate us. How could they not? If I were them I'd hate us too. In fact, I'd hate us even without being them. Take it from me, Rachel, if you just look at us you can see that we deserve nothing but hatred and contempt. And maybe a bit of pity. But that pity cannot come from the Arabs. They themselves need all the pity in the world.

'The devil only knows,' said Pesach Kedem, 'what brought this student who's not really a student here to us. How do we know that he's a student at all? Did you check his certificates before you adopted him? Did you read any of his essays? Did you examine him, in writing or orally? And who says that he's not the one who's digging underneath the house night after night, searching for something, some document or ancient proof that this property once belonged to his forebears? Maybe the reason he came here was that he is scheming to claim some kind of right of return, to establish a claim on the land and the house in the name of some grandfather or great-grandfather who may have lived here in the days of the Ottoman Empire. Or the crusaders. First he moves in here as an uninvited guest, something between a lodger and a servant, he digs under the foundations till the walls start shaking, and then he demands some right, a share in the property, an ancestral claim. And you and I, Rachel, will suddenly find ourselves out in the street. There are flies again on the veranda, there are flies in my room, too. It's those cats of yours, Abigail, that attract the flies. In any case, your cats have taken over the whole house. Your cats, and your Arab, and your beastly vet. And what about us, Rachel? What are we, would you mind telling me that? No? Well, let me tell you then, my dear: we are a passing shadow, like yesterday when it is past.'

Rachel silenced him.

But a moment later she took pity on him and reached for a couple of chocolates wrapped in silver paper from her apron pocket.

'Here, Daddy. Take these. Eat them. Only give me a break.'

9

DANNY FRANCO, dead on his fiftieth birthday, was a sentimental man who was easily moved to tears. He wept at weddings, and sobbed in the films that were shown in the Village Hall. The skin of his neck hung in folds, like a turkey's. He had a soft, guttural way of pronouncing his rs which gave

his speech a hint of a French accent, even though
he hardly knew any French. He was a stocky, broad-
shouldered man, but his legs were spindly: he looked
like a wardrobe set on stick legs. He had a habit
of hugging people he was talking to, even strangers,
patting them on the shoulder, on the chest, between
the ribs, on the back of the neck. He often slapped
his own thighs, too, or gave you an affectionate
punch in the belly.

If somebody praised the way his calves were coming
along, or an omelette he had made, or the beauty of
the sunset from the window of his house, his eyes
immediately filled with moisture in gratitude for the
compliment.

Beneath the stream of words on any subject whatever – the future of calf-fattening, government policy,
a woman's heart, a tractor engine – there always
gushed a stream of joy that had no need of any
pretext or connection. Even on the last day of his
life, ten minutes or so before he dropped dead of
heart failure, he was standing at the fence chatting
to Yossi Sasson and Arieh Zelnik. Most of the time
there was between him and Rachel that ceasefire so
common between couples after long years of

marriage, when conflicts, insults and temporary separations have taught both partners to tread warily and to give the marked minefields a wide berth. From the outside this cautious routine resembled a mutual resignation, which even left room for a calm comradeship, of the type that sometimes develops between soldiers of opposing armies facing each other, a few yards apart, in the course of long-drawn-out trench warfare.

This is how Danny Franco ate an apple: for a while he would turn it around in his hand, inspecting it closely until he found the precise point at which to sink his teeth into it, then he would stare at the wounded apple once more, before attacking it again, this time at another point on its circumference.

After his death Rachel let the farm go. The henhouses were closed, the calves were sold, and the incubator became a storeroom. Rachel continued to water the fruit trees that Danny Franco had planted at the end of the yard, apples and almonds, a couple of dusty fig trees, two pomegranates and an olive. But she gave up pruning the old creepers that clung to the walls of the house, covered the roof and gave shade to the veranda.

The abandoned sheds and outbuildings filled up with junk and dust. Rachel sold the lease on the land further down the slope, and the water ration of the now inoperative farm. She also sold her parental home in Kiryat Tivon, and took in her cantankerous father. With the proceeds of all these sales she bought herself a portfolio of shares and the status of sleeping partner in a small company manufacturing pharmaceutical products and health foods. The company paid her a monthly salary, on top of her pay as literature teacher at Green Meadows High School in Tel Ilan.

10

DESPITE HIS weak body and thin shoulders, Adel took it on himself to weed the former farm-yard, which had become overgrown since Danny's death. He also, of his own initiative, tended a small vegetable patch beside the front path, trimmed and watered the unruly hedge, looked after the olean-ders, roses and geraniums that grew in front of the house, cleaned and tidied the cellar, and did most of the housework, washing floors, hanging out the washing, ironing, and washing the dishes. He even reactivated Danny Franco's little carpentry workshop: he managed to oil and sharpen the electrical saw and get it working again. Rachel bought him a new clamp to replace the old one that was rusted up, some timber, nails, screws and carpenter's glue. In his spare time he made her some shelves and stools, gradually replaced the fence posts, and even removed the old, broken gate and fitted a new one which he painted green. It was a lightweight double gate fitted with springs so that the two flaps swung to and fro behind you several times before closing gently of their own accord, without slamming.

The student spent the long summer evenings sitting on his own on the steps of his hut, which was formerly the hatchery, smoking and writing in a notebook placed on top of a closed book on his knees. Inside the hut Rachel had set him up with an iron bedstead and an old mattress, a school desk and a chair, an electric hotplate, and a small refrigerator where Adel kept some vegetables, cheese, eggs and milk. He stayed sitting on the step until ten or ten-thirty, with a golden cloud of sawdust floating around his dark head in the yellow electric light, his smell of young male sweat mingling with a sharp, heady odour of carpenter's glue

Sometimes he sat there after sunset, playing to himself on a mouth organ, in the twilight or the moonlight.

'There he is again, pouring out his soul with his oriental wailing,' the old man would grumble from the veranda. 'It's probably some song of yearning for our land, which they'll never give up.'

He knew only five or six tunes, but he never tired of repeating them. Sometimes he would stop playing, and sit motionless on the top step, with his back leaning against the side of the shed, deep in thought, or dozing. Around eleven o'clock he would stand up and go inside. The light above his bed would still be on after Rachel and her father had turned out their own bedside lamps and gone to sleep.

'At two o'clock in the morning, when the digging sounds started again,' the old man said, 'I got up and went to check if the little Arab's light was still on. There was no light. He may have turned it off and gone to sleep, but it's just as likely he turned it off and went to dig in our foundations.'

Adel made his own meals: brown bread with slices of tomatoes, olives, cucumber, onion and green pepper, with pieces of salty cheese or sardines, a hard-boiled egg, courgette or aubergine cooked with garlic and tomato sauce, washed down with his favourite drink, which he brewed in a soot-stained tin kettle: hot water and honey, flavoured with some sage leaves and cloves or with rose petals.

Rachel sometimes watched him from the veranda, as he sat on his usual step, with his back leaning against the side of the shed, his notebook on his knees, writing, pausing, thinking, writing a few more words, then pausing again, thinking, writing another line or two, getting up and walking slowly round the yard, turning off a sprinkler, feeding the cats, or scattering a handful of durra for the pigeons. (He had also installed a dovecote at the bottom of the yard.) Then he would sit down again on his step, play his five or six tunes one after the other, eliciting heart-rendingly plaintive, long-drawn-out notes from his harmonica, then wipe the instrument carefully on his shirt-tail and tuck it into his breast pocket. Then he would bend over his notebook again.

Rachel Franco, too, wrote in the evenings. Three

or four times a week, almost every day during that summer, she and her old father sat facing each other on the veranda, on either side of the table that was covered in a flowered oilcloth. The old man talked and talked, while Rachel, frequently pursing her lips, wrote down his memories.

11

'YITZHAK TABENKIN,' Pesach Kedem said, 'better you shouldn't ask me anything about Tabenkin.' (She didn't.) 'When he was an old man Tabenkin decided to disguise himself as a Hasidic rabbi: he grew his beard down to his knees and started issuing rabbinic rulings. But I don't want to say a single word about him. For good or ill. He was a considerable fanatic, believe me, and he was a dogmatist too. A cruel, tyrannical man. He maltreated even his wife and his children all those years. But what is he to me? I have nothing to say about him. You can torture me if you like, you won't get me to say a bad word about Tabenkin. Or a good one either. Kindly note down: Pesach Kedem chooses to maintain a total silence over the whole incident of the great split between him and Tabenkin in 1952. Did you write that down? Word for word? Then kindly add this, too: From an ethical viewpoint, Poalei Zion stood at least two or three rungs below Hapoel Hatza'ir. No. That you should please cross out. Instead you should write: Pesach Kedem no longer sees any reason to become involved in the controversy between Poalei Zion and Hapoel Hatza'ir. It's all over and done with. History has proved both of them wrong, and proved to anyone who is not a fanatic or a dogmatist how wrong they were and how right I was in that controversy. I state this with all due modesty, and with total objectivity: I was right where they both erred. No, cross out "erred" and write "transgressed". And they added iniquity to transgression when they hurled groundless accusations and all sorts of stuff and nonsense at me. But history itself, objective reality, came along and proved in black on white how they had wronged me. And the worst offenders were Comrade Hopeless and Comrade Useless, Tabenkin's cat's paws. Full stop. Yet there was a time, when we were young, that I liked them both. I even liked Tabenkin sometimes, before he became a rabbi. And they liked me up to a point, too. We dreamed of improving ourselves, of improving the whole world. We loved the hills and the valleys, and even the wilderness up to a point. Where were we, Rachel? How did we get here? Where were we before?'

'Tabenkin's beard, I think.'

She filled his glass with Coca-Cola, a drink that he had lately come to be so fond of that it had taken the place for him of both tea and lemonade. Only he insisted on calling it 'Coca-Coca', and nothing his daughter said would make him change. (He also pronounced the names of the two political parties Poalei Zion and Hapoel Hatza'ir, and even his own name, with a marked Yiddish accent.) He insisted on letting the Coca-Cola stand for a while until the bubbles had all subsided before he raised the glass to his cracked lips.

'How about that student of yours,' the old man said suddenly. 'What do you think? He's an anti-semite, isn't he?'

'What makes you say that? What has he done to you?'

'He hasn't done anything. He just doesn't like us. That's all. And why should he?'

After a moment he added:

'I don't like us much myself. There's no reason.'

'Pesach, calm down. Adel lives here and works for us. That's all. He works to pay for his lodging.'

'Wrong!' the old man roared. 'He doesn't work for us, he works instead of us! That's why he digs under the house at night, in the foundations or in the cellar.'

Then he added:

'Cross that out, please. Don't write any of this. Neither what I said against the Arab nor what I said against Tabenkin. At the end of his life Tabenkin was totally senile. Incidentally,' he added, 'even his name was false. The fool was so smitten with the name Tabenkin, Ta-ben-kin – three proletarian hammer blows! Like Cha-lya-pin! Like Marshal Bul-ga-nin! But in fact his original name was simply Toybenkind, Itchele Toybenkind, Itchele Pigeonson! But that little son of a pigeon wanted to be a Molotov! A Stalin! A Hebrew Lenin he wanted to be! *Na*, I don't give a damn about him. I won't say a word about him, for good or ill. Not a word. Abigail, make a note: Pesach Kedem is totally silent on the subject of Tabenkin. A nod is as good as a wink.'

Midges, moths, mosquitoes and daddy-long-legs congregated around the light on the veranda. In the distance, from the direction of the hills, orchards and vineyards, a desperate jackal howled. And opposite, in front of his hut that was lit by a feeble yellow light, Adel got up slowly from his step, stretched, wiped his mouth organ with a cloth, took a few deep breaths, as though trying to draw all the expanse of the night into his narrow chest, and went indoors. Crickets, frogs and sprinklers chirped as if in response to the distant jackal, now joined by a whole choir of jackals somewhere nearby, in the darkened wadi.

'It's getting late,' Rachel said. 'Maybe it's time for us to stop, too, and go indoors?'

'He burrows under our house,' her father said, 'because he simply doesn't like us. Why should he? What for? Because of all our villainy, our cruelty, our arrogance? And our hypocrisy?'

'Who doesn't like us?'

'Him. The goy.'

'Daddy, that's enough now. He's got a name. Please use it. When you talk about him you sound like the last of the antisemites yourself.'

'The last of the antisemites hasn't been born yet. And never will be.'

'Come to bed, Pesach.'

'I don't like him either. Not one bit. I don't like all they've done to us, and to themselves. And I certainly don't like what they want to do to us. And I don't like the way he looks at us, in that hungry, mocking way. He looks at you hungrily, and he looks at me contemptuously.'

'Goodnight. I'm going to bed.'

'So what if I don't like him? Nobody likes anybody, anyway.'

'Goodnight. Don't forget to take your pills before you go to sleep.'

'Once, a long time ago, before all this, maybe here and there some people liked each other a bit. Not everyone. Not much. Not always. Just here and there, a little bit. But now? These days? Now all the hearts are dead. It's finished.'

'There are mosquitoes, Daddy. Would you mind closing the door.'

'Why are all the hearts dead? Maybe you know? Do you?'

12

IN THE night, at two or two-thirty, woken again by tapping, scraping and digging sounds, the old man got out of bed (he always slept in his long johns), and felt for the torch he had put out specially and the iron bar he had found in one of the sheds, his feet groping in the dark like blind beggars for his slippers. Giving these up in despair he padded barefoot into the corridor, feeling the walls and furniture with a trembling hand, his head thrust forward at its characteristic right angle. He finally found the cellar door and pulled it towards him, but the door was made to be pushed open, not pulled, and the iron bar slipped out of his grasp and fell on his foot and to the floor with a dull metallic clang that failed to wake Rachel but did silence the digging sounds.

The old man switched on his torch, bent over with a groan and picked up the iron bar. His bent body cast three or four distorted shadows on the walls of the corridor, on the floor, and on the kitchen door.

He stood there for a few minutes, with the bar under his arm, one hand holding the torch and the other tugging on the cellar door, and straining to hear, but since the silence was deep and complete, punctuated only by the sounds of cicadas and frogs, he reconsidered and decided to go back to bed and try again the following night.

He woke again before dawn and sat up in bed, but he did not reach out for the torch and the bar because this time total silence filled the night. Pesach Kedem sat in bed for a while, listening attentively to the deep silence. Even the cicadas had stopped. There was only a very fine breeze stirring the tops of the cypress trees bordering the cemetery, but it was too faint for him to hear, and he curled up and fell asleep.

13

NEXT MORNING, before going off to school, Rachel went outside to take the old man's trousers off the washing line. Adel was waiting for her by the dovecote, with his glasses that were too small for him, his shy smile that put a dimple in his cheek, and his Van Gogh-style straw hat.

'Rachel. Excuse me. It won't take a moment.'

'Good morning, Adel. Don't forget to straighten that crooked paving stone at the end of the path. Somebody could trip over it.'

'OK, Rachel. But I wanted to ask you what happened in the night.'

'In the night? What happened in the night?'

'I thought maybe you knew. Do you have men working in the yard at night?'

'Working? In the night?'

'Didn't you hear anything? At two o'clock in the morning? Noises? Digging? You must be a very sound sleeper.'

'What sort of noises?'

'Noises down below, Rachel.'

'You were just dreaming, Adel. Who would come and dig underneath your room in the middle of the night?'

'I don't know. I thought maybe you would know.'

'You were dreaming. Remember to fix that paving stone today, before Pesach trips over it and has a fall.'

'I was thinking, maybe your dad walks around at night. Maybe he has trouble sleeping? Maybe he gets up, picks up a shovel, and starts digging?'

'Don't talk nonsense, Adel. No one's digging. You were dreaming.'

She walked back towards the house, carrying the laundry she had taken off the line, but the student went on standing there for a while, watching her walking away. He took off his glasses and polished them on his shirt tail. Then he walked towards the cypresses in his clumsy big shoes, and coming across one of Rachel's cats he bent down and spoke a few sentences to it, in Arabic, respectfully, as though the two of them now had to shoulder a new, serious responsibility.

14

THE SCHOOL year was coming to an end. The summer was getting hotter. The pale blue light turned at midday to a dazzling white glare that hung over the houses and oppressed the gardens and orchards, the red-hot tin huts and closed wooden shutters. A hot, dry wind blew from the hills. The inhabitants of the village stayed indoors during the day and only came out onto their verandas and terraces at dusk. The evenings were warm and humid. Rachel and her father slept with their windows and shutters open. Distant barking in the night stirred bands of jackals to bitter wailing from the direction of the wadi. Sounds of far-off shooting came from beyond the hills. Choirs of cicadas and frogs loaded the night air with a dull, monotonous weight. At midnight Adel went and turned off the sprinklers. Because the heat stopped him sleeping, he sat on his step and smoked a few more cigarettes in the dark.

Sometimes Rachel was full of anger and impatience, at her father, at the house and yard, at the depressing village, at the way her life was being wasted here among yawning schoolchildren and her demanding father. How much longer would she be stuck here? She could simply get up and go some day, hire a carer to look after her father and leave the student to look after the yard and the house. She could go back to university and finally finish her thesis on moments of illumination and revelation in the writings of Yizhar and Kahana-Carmon, she could renew old friendships, travel, go and see Osnat in Brussels, Yifat in America, she could give her life a makeover. There were moments when she was startled because she caught herself daydreaming of the old man falling victim to some domestic tragedy: a fall, electrocution, gas.

Every evening Rachel Franco and ex-MK Pesach Kedem sat on the veranda, where they had installed an electric fan with an extension lead. Rachel would be busy with marking, while the old man leafed through some magazine or pamphlet, turning the pages backwards and forwards, grumbling and growling, swearing and cursing at the hotheads and imbeciles. Or alternatively full of self-loathing, calling himself a cruel tyrant, making up his mind to ask for forgiveness from Micky the vet: why did I mock him, why did I nearly throw him out of the house last week? After all, he does his job conscientiously, at least. I could have become a vet myself, instead of becoming an apparatchik, and then I could have brought some good into the world, I could have managed occasionally to reduce the amount of pain round here.

Sometimes the old man dozed with his mouth

open, breathing stertorously, his white moustache stirring as though endowed with a secret life of its own. When Rachel got through her marking, she might pick up the brown notebook and take down her father's account of the tragic rift between the majority faction and Group B, or his description of his own position during the Great Split, how right he had been and how wrong were the various false prophets and how differently things might have turned out if only both sides had listened to him.

They did not discuss the nocturnal digging sounds. The old man had made his mind up to catch the miscreants red-handed, while Rachel had developed an explanation of her own of her father's and Adel's disturbed nights: the former was half-deaf and heard noises inside his own head, while the latter was a nervous and perhaps even slightly neurotic young man, with a highly developed imagination. It was possible, Rachel thought, that some distant sounds came in the early hours of the morning from one of the neighbouring properties: perhaps they were milking the cows, and the noise of the milking machine coupled with the sound of the metal gate opening and closing as the cows went through might have sounded, in these oppressive summer nights, like the noise of digging. Or they might both have heard in their sleep the sound of the old, worn-out drains that ran under the house.

One morning, while Adel was doing the ironing in Rachel's bedroom, the old man suddenly pounced on him, with his head thrust forward like a charging bull, and began to interrogate him:

'So, you're a student, eh? What sort of student are you then?'

'I'm an arts student.'

'Arts, huh? What art exactly? The art of talking nonsense? The art of deception? The dark arts? And if you are indeed an arts student, then tell me this if you don't mind: what are you doing here, why aren't you at university?

'I'm taking a break from university. I'm trying to write a book about you.'

'About us?'

'About you, and about us. A comparison.'

'A comparison. What sort of a comparison? A comparison to show that we are the robbers and you are the robbed? To reveal our ugly face?'

'Not ugly, exactly. More like unhappy.'

'And how about your face? Isn't it unhappy? Are you so pretty? Beyond reproach? Saintly and pure?'

'We're unhappy too.'

'So there's no difference between us? If that's the case, why are you sitting here writing a comparison?'

'There are some differences.'

'Like what, for example?'

Adel skilfully folded the blouse he was ironing, carefully laid it on the bed, placed another one on the ironing board, and sprinkled some water on it from a bottle before starting to iron.

'Our unhappiness is partly our fault and partly your fault. But your unhappiness comes from your soul.'

'Our soul?'

'Or from your heart. It's hard to know. It comes from you. From inside. The unhappiness. It comes from deep inside you.'

'Tell me please, Comrade Adel, since when do Arabs play the harmonica?'

'A friend of mine taught me. A Russian friend. And a girl gave it to me as a present.'

'And why are you always playing sad tunes? Are you miserable here?'

'It's like this: whatever one plays on the harmonica, from a distance it always sounds sad. It's like you, from a distance you seem to be sad.'

'And from close up?'

'From close up you seem to me more like an angry man. And now, please excuse me, I've finished the ironing and now I need to feed the pigeons.'

'Mister Adel.'

'Yes?'

'Please tell me, why are you digging under the cellar at night? It is you, isn't it? What are you hoping to find there?'

'What, do you hear noises at night, too? How come Rachel doesn't hear them? She doesn't hear them and she doesn't believe they exist. Doesn't she believe you either?'

15

RACHEL DID not believe either in her father's nocturnal imaginings or in Adel's dreams. Both of them probably heard the sounds of milking from one of the neighbouring farms or the army on night manoeuvres in the farmland on the slopes of the hills, and translated these sounds in their imaginations into sounds of digging. Nevertheless, she decided to stay awake one night into the early hours so as to hear with her own ears.

Meanwhile the last days of term arrived. The older pupils were busy with feverish revision for the exams, while in the middle classes discipline was deteriorating: the students were late for class, and some were absent on various excuses. The classes seemed poorly attended and restless, and she herself taught her last lessons wearily. Several times she let a class off the last quarter of an hour and sent the pupils out into the playground early. Once or twice, by special request, she agreed to devote the time to a free discussion on a subject suggested by her pupils.

On Saturdays the narrow lanes of the village filled with visitors' cars that were parked between fences and blocked the entrances. Crowds of bargain-hunters thronged round the homemade cheese stalls, the spice shops and the boutique wineries, the farm-yards selling Indian furniture and ornaments from Burma and Bangladesh, the stores selling oriental rugs and carpets and the art galleries, all those activities the village had turned to as agriculture was gradually abandoned, even though some farms still fattened calves, hatched chicks or grew houseplants in hothouses, and vines and fruit trees still covered the slopes of the hills.

As Rachel walked briskly down the road on her way to school and back again people looked at her and wondered about her strange life, between her elderly parliamentarian and her Arab youth. Other farms too had hired workers, Thais, Romanians, Arabs and Chinese, but at Rachel Franco's nothing grew and no ornaments or artworks were made. So why did she need this workman? And an intellectual, too? From the university? Micky the vet, who played draughts with the Arab worker, had said that he was some kind of student? Or bookworm?

Some said one thing, others another. Micky the vet himself stated that he had seen this Arab boy with his own eyes ironing and folding her underwear, and that he didn't only hang around the yard but actually had the freedom of the house, like a family member. The old man talked to him about the splits in the labour movement, and the Arab chatted with all the cats, repaired the roof, and gave recitals on the harmonica every evening.

People in the village had fond memories of Danny Franco, dead of heart failure on his fiftieth birthday. Thickset, broad-shouldered with his matchstick legs, he was a warm-hearted man, who behaved affectionately towards other people, and was not embarrassed about it. He wept on the morning of the day he died because a calf was dying on the farm. Or because one of the cats had given birth to two stillborn kittens. At midday his heart failed and he collapsed on his back outside the fertiliser store. Rachel found him there, with an expression of surprised outrage on his face, as though he had been thrown off some course in the army for no reason. At first Rachel couldn't understand why he was taking a nap in the middle of the day, lying on the ground on his back next to the shed, and she shouted at him, Danny, what's the matter with you, get up now, stop behaving like a child. It was only when she took hold of his hands to help him up that she realised they were cold. She bent over him and tried mouth-to-mouth resuscitation; she even slapped his cheeks. Then she ran into the house to ring the village clinic, to summon Dr Gili Steiner. Her voice barely shook and her eyes were dry. She regretted slapping his face for no reason.

16

IT WAS a hot, humid evening, the trees in the garden were wrapped in a damp vapour, and even the stars seemed to be immersed in dirty cotton wool. Rachel Franco was sitting on the veranda with her old father, reading an Israeli novel about the residents of a block of flats in Tel Aviv. The old man, his black military beret pulled down over his forehead, his baggy khaki trousers held up by braces, turned the pages of the supplements of *Haaretz*, mouthing angry rants as he did so. 'Poor wretches,' he mumbled, 'they're really out of luck, lonely to the marrow of their bones, abandoned from their mothers' wombs, no one can stand them. No one can stand anyone any more. Everyone is a stranger to everyone else. Even the stars in the sky are alien to one another.'

Thirty yards away from them Adel was sitting on the top step of his hut, smoking as he calmly repaired a pair of secateurs whose spring had come loose. Two cats lay on the parapet of the veranda as though fainting in the heat. From the depths of the hazy night came the chugging sound of a sprinkler and the drawn-out grating of crickets. Every now and again a night bird uttered a piercing shriek. And in faraway farmyards dogs were barking, with a sound that sometimes descended to a sad, heart-rending howl answered occasionally by the wail of a solitary jackal from the orchards on the slopes of the hill. Rachel raised her eyes from her book and said, to herself rather than to her father:

'Sometimes I ask myself what on earth I am doing here.'

'Of course,' said the old man. 'I know I'm a burden on you.'

'I'm not talking about you, Pesach, I'm talking about my own life. Why do you bring everything straight back to yourself?'

'So please, go off,' the old man chuckled, 'go and find yourself a new life. I'll stay on here with the little Arab to look after the garden and the house. Until it falls down. It won't be long before it collapses on top of us.'

'Falls down? Until what falls down?'

'The house. Those diggers are undermining the foundations.'

'Nobody is digging. I'm going to buy you some earplugs so that you don't wake up in the night.'

Adel put down the secateurs, stubbed out his cigarette, pulled out his mouth organ and played a few hesitant notes as if he couldn't decide which tune to play. Or as if he were trying to imitate the desperate wailing of the jackal that came from the direction of the orchards. And the jackal really did seem to respond from the darkness. A plane flew high above the village, its wing lights flashing. The suffocating air was damp and warm and dense, almost solid.

'That's a lovely tune,' the old man said. 'Heart-rending. It reminds us of a time when there was still some fleeting affection between people. There's no point in playing tunes like that today: they are an anachronism, because nobody cares any more. That's all over. Now our hearts are blocked. All feelings are dead. Nobody turns to anyone else except from self-interested motives. What is left? Maybe only this melancholy tune, as a kind of reminder of the destruction of our hearts.'

Rachel poured three glasses of lemon squash and called to Adel to come and join them on the veranda. The old man asked for Coca-Cola instead, but this time he didn't insist. Adel came over, with his little boy's glasses hanging on a cord round his neck, and sat down to one side, on the stone parapet. Rachel asked him to play for them. Adel hesitated, then chose a Russian tune, full of longing and sorrow. His friends at Haifa University had taught him these Russian tunes. The old man stopped grumbling and extended his tortoise neck at an angle, as though trying to move his good ear closer to the source of the music. Then he sighed and said:

'Oh, to hell with it. What a pity.'

But he didn't bother to explain what was a pity this time.

At ten past eleven Rachel says she is feeling tired, and asks Adel some question about the next day, something about sawing off a branch or painting a bench. Adel softly promises and asks a couple of questions. Rachel replies. The old man folds his newspaper: in two, in four, in eight, until it makes a little square. Rachel stands and picks up the tray with the fruit and biscuits, but leaves them the glasses and the bottle. She tells her father not to go to bed too late, and reminds Adel to switch off the light when he leaves. Then she wishes them both goodnight, steps over a couple of sleeping cats, and goes indoors. The old man nods a few times, and mutters after her, into empty space rather than to Adel:

'Well, yes. She needs a change. We tire her out so.'

17

RACHEL GOES to her bedroom. She switches on the ceiling light, then turns on her bedside lamp instead. She stands in front of the open window for a few moments. The night air is warm and close and the stars are surrounded by patches of haze. The crickets are in full voice. The sprinklers are swishing. She listens to the sounds of the jackals in the hills and the answering barking of the dogs in the yards. She turns her back to the window, without closing it, takes off her dress, scratches herself, finishes undressing and puts on a short cotton night-dress printed with little flowers. She pours herself a glass of water and drinks some. She goes to the toilet. When she returns she stands at the window again for a while. She can hear the old man on the veranda talking angrily to Adel, and Adel replying briefly in his soft voice. She can't catch what they are saying, and she wonders what the old man wants from the youth this time and also what it is that keeps the youth here.

A mosquito buzzes beside her ear. And a moth dances drunkenly round her bedside lamp, crashing into the bulb. She is suddenly sorry for herself and feels sad for the days that go by so aimlessly and pointlessly. The school year is ending, then it will be the summer holidays, and then another year will begin, no different from the one that is ending. More marking, more staff meetings, more Micky the vet.

Rachel switches on the fan and gets under the sheet. But she is not tired any more; instead she feels wide awake. She pours some more water from the bottle on her bedside table, drinks, turns restlessly,

117

puts a pillow between her legs, and turns again. A faint, almost inaudible grating sound makes her sit up and switch on her bedside light. Now she can hear no sound except the crickets, the frogs, the sprinklers and the distant dogs. She turns out the light, pushes off the sheet, and lies on her back. And then something starts grating again, as though the floor tiles are being scraped with a nail.

Rachel turns on the light and gets out of bed. She checks the shutter, but it is open and firmly anchored. She checks the curtain too, in case the noise came from there, and the door of the toilet, but there is no breeze. Not even a faint one. She sits on a chair for a while but she hears no sound. As soon as she gets back into bed, covers herself with the sheet and turns off the light, the gnawing sounds again. Is there a mouse in the room? It's hard to imagine, because the house is overrun with cats. Now she has the impression that someone is scratching the floor under her bed with a sharp instrument. She freezes and holds her breath, straining to listen: now the scratching is punctuated with faint knocking or tapping sounds. She switches the bedside light on again and gets down on hands and knees to look under the bed: there is nothing there, apart from some dust-balls and a scrap of paper. Rachel does not get back into bed, but stands, alert, in the centre of the room, after switching the ceiling light on too. Now, even with the light on, she can hear the gnawing and scratching sounds, and she decides that someone, perhaps Adel or more likely her terrible old man, is bending down outside her window and deliberately scraping the wall and tapping on it lightly. Neither of them is entirely sane. She takes the torch from the shelf beside her wardrobe and prepares to go round to the back of the house. Or should she go down to the cellar?

First, though, she goes out on the veranda to see which of them is not sitting there, so that she will know whom to suspect. But the veranda is in darkness and the old man's window is dark too. So is Adel's hut. Rachel, in her sandals and nightdress, goes round to the side of the house, stoops between the pillars that support the house, and shines the torch into the space under her floor: it lights dusty cobwebs, and alarms an insect that scuttles away into the darkness. She straightens up and stands surrounded by the deep stillness of the night.

Nothing stirs the row of cypresses separating her yard from the cemetery. There is no hint of a breeze. Even the crickets and the dogs have momentarily fallen silent. The darkness is dense and oppressive, and the heat hangs heavily over everything. Rachel Franco stands there trembling alone in the dark under the blurred stars.

Lost

1

I HAD a phone call yesterday from Batya Rubin, the widow of Eldad Rubin. She didn't beat about the bush, she simply asked if she was speaking to Yossi Sasson, the estate agent, and when I replied, 'At your service, ma'am,' she said, 'It's time for us to talk.'

I've had my eye for a long time on the Rubins' house in Tarpat (1929) Street, behind the Pioneers' Garden, the house that we call The Ruin. It's an old house, built not long after the village was founded, more than a century ago. The other old houses that used to stand on either side of it, the Wilenski House and the Shmueli House, have been demolished and replaced by villas several storeys high. These villas are surrounded by well-kept gardens and one of them even has an ornamental pond, complete with artificial waterfall, goldfish and fountain. The Ruin stands between them like a black tooth in a row of white teeth. It's a big, rambling house with all sorts of wings and extensions, built of sandstone, and most of the plaster has peeled off. It has a withdrawn air, standing back from the road, turning its back to the world and surrounded by an unkempt yard full of thistles and rusting junk. A blocked well stands in the middle, topped by a corroded hand-pump. The windows are always shuttered, and the paved path leading from the gate to the house is overgrown with convolvulus, prosopis and couch grass. A few blouses and items of underwear that can occasionally be seen hanging from the washing line at the side of the house are the only signs of life.

For many years we had a well-known writer here in Tel Ilan, Eldad Rubin, an invalid in a wheelchair who wrote long novels about the Holocaust, even though he had spent all his life in Tel Ilan apart from a few years studying in Paris in the late Fifties. He was born here in this old house in Tarpat Street, he wrote all his books here, and it was here that he died about ten years ago, at the age of fifty-nine. Ever since his death I have been hoping to buy the house and sell it on for demolition and rebuilding. As a matter of fact I have tried to read Eldad Rubin's books once or twice but they weren't my sort of thing: everything in them seems so heavy and depressing, the plots are so slow, and the characters so wretched. I mostly read the economic supplements of the paper, political books and thrillers.

Two women live in The Ruin and so far they have refused to sell at any price: Rosa, the writer's ninety-five-year-old mother, and his widow, who must be in her sixties. I've tried phoning them a few times, and it's always the widow, Batya, who answers. I always begin by expressing my admiration for the late writer's books, which are a source of pride to the entire village, continue with some hints about the dilapidated condition of the property, suggesting that there's no point in doing it up, and end with a polite request to be invited for a brief discussion about the future. The conversation invariably ends with Batya Rubin thanking me for my interest but stating that as the matter is not currently on their agenda, there would be no point in my going round to see them.

Until yesterday, when she rang of her own accord and said, 'It's time for us to talk.' I made up my mind immediately not to start bringing purchasers to her but to buy The Ruin myself. Then I'd have it demolished, and I'd get more for the site than I'd paid for the house. I was inside the house once when I was little. My mother, who was a registered nurse, took me with her when she was called out to give an injection to the writer Eldad Rubin. I was nine or ten. I remember a spacious central room furnished in oriental style, from which a lot of doors opened off, as well as some stairs that appeared to go down to a cellar. The furniture looked heavy and dark. Two of the walls were lined with bookshelves from floor to ceiling, and another was covered with maps studded with different-coloured drawing pins. A vase on the table contained a bunch of thistles. And the ticking of a grandfather clock with gilded hands beat time.

The writer himself was sitting in his wheelchair, a tartan rug covering his knees and his big head framed by a mane of grey hair. I can remember a broad red face sunk between his shoulders, as though he had no neck, and his large ears, and bushy eyebrows that were also turning grey. There were grey hairs protruding from his ears and nostrils, too. There was something about him that reminded me of a hibernating bear. My mother and his mother hauled him from the wheelchair to the sofa, and he didn't make it any easier for them by grumbling and growling and struggling to escape, but his muscles were too weak and they got the better of him. His mother Rosa pulled down his trousers until his swollen buttocks were exposed and my mother bent over and gave him the injection in the top of his white thigh. Afterwards the writer joked with her. I can't remember what he said, but I do remember that it wasn't very funny. Then his wife, Batya, came in. She was a thin, nervy woman with her hair gathered in a little bun. She offered my mother a glass of tea, and gave me some sweetish black-currant juice in a cup that seemed to me to be cracked. My mother and I sat for about a quarter of an hour in the sitting room of the house which was already referred to in the village as The Ruin. And I remember there was something about the house that captured my imagination. Perhaps it was the fact that five or six doors opened off that central room, straight into the rooms surrounding it. That wasn't the way the houses in our village were built. I have only ever seen this style of building in Arab villages. The writer himself, even though, as I knew, he wrote books about the Holocaust, didn't seem at all gloomy or mournful but radiated a sort of forced boyish gaiety. He tried hard to entertain us in his sleepy way, telling us anecdotes, amusing himself with plays on words, but I remember him from that single meeting not as a charming man but as someone who was making a huge effort to ensure everything went off as pleasantly as possible.

2

AT SIX o'clock in the evening I got up from my desk and went out for a walk round the village. I was tired and my eyes were aching from a long day at the office, a day given over to preparing the annual tax return. I meant to walk for half an hour or an hour, have something light to eat at Chaimowicz's restaurant, then go back to my work, which had to be finished by that night. I was so tired that the evening light didn't seem totally clear, but somehow cloudy or dusty. It was a hot, humid summer's day in Tel Ilan. At the end of Well Street there is a wall of cypress trees behind which is a pear orchard. The sun was beginning to sink behind the cypresses on its course towards the western horizon. The sun looked tarnished at the close of this torrid June day, a greyish veil between us and it. I was walking at an average pace, neither slowly nor fast. Now and again I paused and gazed distractedly into a front yard. There were only a few people in the streets, hurrying home. At this time of day most of the village folk generally sit indoors or on their rear verandas facing the garden, dressed in singlet and shorts, sipping iced lemonade and leafing through the evening paper.

A few passers-by crossed my path. Avraham Levin nodded a greeting, and one or two others stopped to exchange a few words. Here in the village we almost all know one another. Some people resent my buying up the houses in the village and selling them to outsiders who build themselves weekend homes or holiday villas. Soon the village won't be a village any more, it'll turn into a sort of summer resort. The older inhabitants are unhappy about this change, even though the newcomers have made the village rich and turned it from a forgotten bywater into a place bustling with life, at least at weekends. Every Saturday queues of cars arrive in the village, and their passengers visit the boutique wineries, the art galleries, the stores selling Far Eastern furnishings, and the cheese, honey and olive stalls.

In the hot evening twilight I reached the open square in front of the Village Hall in Founders' Street, and my feet led me behind the building, to a dismal empty space where a garden has been planted pointlessly, since no one ever comes to this forsaken spot. I stood here for a few minutes waiting, though I had no idea who or what I was waiting for. A dusty little statue stands here, surrounded by yellow grass and a bed of thirsty roses, in memory of five of the founders of the village who were killed in an attack a hundred years ago. By the back door of the hall was a noticeboard advertising an unforgettable evening with three musicians who were coming the next weekend. Underneath the poster was another from some religious missionaries, declaring that this world is merely a gloomy antechamber in which we must prepare ourselves to enter the Sanctuary. I stared at it for a few minutes, reflecting that I knew nothing of the Sanctuary, but that I quite enjoyed the antechamber.

While I was looking at the noticeboard a woman, who a moment ago had not been there, appeared

next to the statue. She looked odd and even faintly
bizarre in the evening light. Had she come out of the
rear entrance of the hall? Or had she come through
the narrow passageway between the adjacent buildings? It seemed uncanny to me that a moment ago I
was all alone here and suddenly this strange woman
had materialised out of nowhere. She was not from
here. She was slim and erect, with an aquiline nose
and a short, solid neck, and on her head she was
wearing a weird, yellow hat covered in buckles and
brooches. She was dressed in khaki like a hiker, with
a red haversack over one shoulder, a water bottle
attached to her belt, and heavy walking shoes. She
was holding a stick in one hand, and over the other
arm was draped a raincoat that was definitely out of
place in June. She looked as if she had stepped out
of a foreign advertisement for nature walks. Not here,
but in some cooler country. I couldn't tear my eyes
away from her.

The strange woman looked back at me sharply,
with an almost hostile air. She stood haughtily, as
if she despised me wholeheartedly or as if she were
trying to signify that there was no hope for me and
we were both well aware of it. So piercing was her

gaze that I had no choice but to look away and move off quickly in the direction of Founders' Street and the front of the Village Hall. After ten or so paces I couldn't stop myself turning round. She wasn't there. The ground seemed to have opened up and swallowed her. But my mind wouldn't settle. I walked round the Village Hall and continued up Founders' Street with a persistent feeling that something was wrong, that there was something I had to do, something serious and important, that it was my duty to do but that I was avoiding.

So I walked to The Ruin to talk right away to the widow, Batya Rubin, and perhaps also to Rosa Rubin, the old mother. After all, they had finally contacted me at the office to say that it was time for us to talk.

3

As I walked I thought that it was rather a pity to demolish The Ruin. It was, after all, one of the last of the original houses built by the founders more than a hundred years ago. The writer Eldad

Rubin's grandfather was a well-off farmer named
Gedalya Rubin, who was among the first settlers in
Tel Ilan. He built himself a house with his own hands,
and he planted a fruit orchard and also a successful
vineyard. He was known in the village as a tight-
fisted, short tempered farmer. His wife, Martha, was
known in her youth as the prettiest girl in the
Menasseh District. But The Ruin was so decrepit and
run-down that there was no point in spending money
restoring and renovating it. I was still contemplating
purchasing it from the mother and the widow and
selling the site for the building of a new villa. It might
be possible to arrange for a commemorative plaque
to be fixed to the façade of the new building, saying
that on this spot once stood the home of the writer
Eldad Rubin, and it was here that he wrote all his
books about the horrors of the Holocaust. When I
was a little boy I used to think that these horrors
were still going on somehow inside the writer's house,
in the cellar or in one of the back rooms.

In the little square by the bus stop I bumped
into Benny Avni, the village Mayor. He was standing
there with the chief engineer and a paving contractor
from Netanya, talking to them about replacing the

old paving stones. I was surprised to see them standing there confabulating at this twilight hour. Benny Avni slapped me on the shoulder and said:

'How are you doing, Mister Estate Agent?'

Then he said: 'You look a bit worried, Yossi.' And he added: 'Pop into my office when you have a moment, maybe on Friday afternoon, you and I need to have a word.'

But when I put some feelers out about what we needed to have a word about I couldn't extract the slightest hint from him.

'Come,' he said, 'we'll talk, coffee's on me.'

This exchange heightened my sense of disquiet: something that I ought to be doing, or to refrain from doing, weighed on me and clouded my thoughts, but what that thing was I could not think. So I set off for The Ruin. But I didn't go straight there, I made a slight detour, via the school and the avenue of pine trees next to it. It suddenly struck me that the strange woman who had appeared to me in that out-of-the-way garden behind the Village Hall had been trying to give me some sort of a clue, maybe a vitally important hint, which I had refused to take heed of. What was it that had scared me so? Why had I run away from her? But had I really run away? After all, when I turned back to look, she wasn't there. It was as though she had faded into the evening twilight. A thin, erect figure dressed in strange travelling gear, with a walking stick in one hand and a folded raincoat draped over her other arm. As though it were not June. She had looked to me like a hiker in the Alps. Maybe Austrian. Or Swiss? What had she been trying to say to me and why had I felt the need to get away from her? I could find no answer to these questions, nor could I imagine what it was that Benny Avni wanted to talk to me about or why he couldn't simply raise the matter when we had met in the little square by the bus stop, but had invited me to call on him in his office at such a strange time, on Friday afternoon.

A smallish package wrapped in brown paper and tied up with black cord was lying on a shady bench at the end of Tarpat Street. I paused and bent over to see what was written on it. There was nothing written on it. I picked it up cautiously and turned it over but the brown paper was smooth and unmarked. After a moment's hesitation I decided not to open the package, but felt I ought to let someone know

I had found it. I didn't know whom I should tell. I held it in both my hands and it seemed heavier than its size would have suggested, heavier than a packet of books, as if it contained stones or metal. Now the object aroused my suspicion, and so I replaced it gently on the bench. I ought to have reported the discovery of a suspicious package to the police, but my mobile phone was on my desk at the office because I had only gone out for a short walk and didn't want to be interrupted by office business.

Meanwhile, the last light was slowly fading, and only the afterglow of the sunset was still shimmering at the bottom of the road, beckoning to me or else warning me to keep away. The street was filling with deeper shadows, from the tall cypress trees and the fences surrounding the front gardens of the properties. The shadows did not stand still, but moved to and fro, as though bending down to look for something that was lost. After a few moments the street lights came on; the shadows did not retreat, but mingled with the light breeze that was moving the treetops as if an unseen hand were stirring and blending them.

I stopped at the broken iron gate of The Ruin, and

stood there for a few minutes, inhaling the scent of the oleanders and the bitter smell of the geraniums. The house seemed to be empty, as there was no light in any of the windows or in the garden, just the sound of the crickets among the thistles and the frogs in the neighbouring garden, and the persistent barking of dogs from further down the street. Why had I come here without ringing first to make an appointment? If I knocked on the door now, after dark, the two women would be bound to be alarmed. They might not even open the door. But perhaps they were both out – there was no light in the windows. So I decided to leave and come back another day. But, while I was still making up my mind, I opened the gate, which creaked ominously, crossed the dark front garden, and knocked twice on the front door.

4

THE DOOR was opened by Yardena, the daughter of the late Eldad Rubin, a young woman of about twenty-five. Her mother and grandmother had gone to Jerusalem and she had come from Haifa to be on her own for a few days and get on with her seminar paper on the founders of Tel Ilan. I remembered Yardena from her childhood, because once, when she was about twelve, she came to my office, sent by her father, to ask for a plan of the village. She was a bashful, fair-haired girl, with a beanstalk body and long thin neck, and delicate features that seemed full of wonderment, as though everything that happened surprised her and afforded her shy puzzlement. I had tried to engage her in a little conversation about her father, his books, the visitors who came to them from all over the country, but she would only answer yes and no and at one point she said, 'How would I know?' And so our conversation was over before it had begun. I handed her the plan of the village that her father had requested, and she thanked me and went out, leaving behind a trail of shyness and surprise, as if she had found me or my office amazing. Since then I'd bumped into her a few times at Victor Ezra's grocery shop, at the council offices or at the health clinic, and each time she had smiled at me like an old friend but said little. She always left me with a sense of frustration, as though there were some conversation between us that hadn't yet taken place. Six or seven years ago she had been called up for military service, and after that, people said, she had gone off to study in Haifa.

Now she was standing in front of me at the entrance to this shuttered house, a graceful, fragile looking young woman, in a plain cotton frock, with loose, flowing hair, wearing white socks with her sandals like a schoolgirl. I lowered my eyes and looked only at her sandals. 'Your mother rang me,' I said, 'and asked me round to talk about the future of the house.'

That was when Yardena told me that her mother and grandmother had gone to Jerusalem for a few days and she was alone in the house, but she invited me in, even though it was no good talking to her about the future of the house. I made up my mind to thank her, take my leave and come back another day, but my feet followed her into the house of their own accord. I entered the large room I remembered from my childhood, that high-ceilinged room from which various doors opened onto side rooms and steps led down into the cellar. The room was lit by a faint golden light filtered by metal lampshades fixed close to the ceiling. Two of the walls were lined with shelves laden with books, while the east wall still carried a large map of the Mediterranean lands. The map had begun to turn yellow and its edges were tattered. There was something old and dense in the room, a faint smell of things that had not been aired, or maybe it wasn't a smell but the golden light catching tiny specks of dust that shimmered in a diagonal column above the dark dining table flanked by eight straight-backed dining chairs.

Yardena sat me down in an old mauve-coloured armchair and asked me what I would like to eat.

'Please don't go to any trouble,' I said, 'I don't want to disturb you, I'll just sit and rest for a few minutes and I'll come back another time, when your mother and your grandmother are at home.'

Yardena insisted that I ought to have something to drink. 'It's so hot today, and you walked here,' she said. As she left the room I looked at her long legs with their little girl's sandals and white socks. Her dark blue dress just skimmed her knees. There was a deep silence in the house, as though it had already been sold and vacated for ever. An old-fashioned wall clock ticked above the sofa, and outside a dog was barking in the distance, but no breeze stirred the tops

140

of the cypresses that surrounded the house on all sides. A full moon was visible in the east window. The dark patches on the surface of the moon looked darker than usual.

When Yardena returned I noticed that she had removed her sandals and socks and was now barefoot. She was holding a black glass tray on which were a single glass, a bottle of cold water, and a plate of dates, plums and cherries. The bottle was beaded with icy perspiration, and the glass had a thin blue line running round it. She put the tray down in front of me, leant over and filled the glass with water up to the blue line. As she bent over I caught a glimpse of the mounds of her breasts and the cleft between them. Her breasts were small and firm and for a moment I thought they looked like the fruit she had served me. I took five or six sips and touched the fruit with my fingers but I didn't take any, though the plums were also covered in condensation, or droplets of water from washing, and looked tasty and tempting. I told Yardena that I could remember her father and that I recalled this room from my childhood, and almost nothing in it had changed. She said that her father had loved this house, where he had been born and raised and where he had written all his books, but that her mother wanted to leave and live in the city. She found the silence oppressive. Apparently her grandmother would be put into a home and the house would be sold. It was her mother's business. If she was asked for her opinion she might say that the sale should be postponed so long as her grandmother was alive. But on the other hand you could understand her mother's point of view: why should she stay on here now that she had retired from her job as a biology teacher in the school? She was alone here all the time with the old lady, who was getting hard of hearing.

'Would you like to see over the house? Shall I give you a tour? There are so many rooms. This house was built without any rhyme or reason,' Yardena said. 'As if the architect got carried away, and built whatever rooms and passages he had a mind to. In fact he wasn't even an architect: my great-grandfather built the main part of the house and every few years he added a new wing, and then my grandfather came along and built more extensions and more rooms.'

I got up and followed her through one of the doors that led into the dark, and found myself in a stone-paved passageway lined with old photographs of hills and streams. My eyes were fixed on her bare feet, that moved nimbly over the flagstones, as if she were dancing in front of me. Several doors opened off this passageway, and Yardena said that even though she had grown up in the house she still had a feeling that she was in a maze, and there were corners she had not been in since she was small. She opened one of the doors and we went down five steps into a dark, winding passage lit only by a single feeble bulb. Here, too, there were glass-fronted cabinets filled with old books, interspersed with a collection of fossils and sea shells. Yardena said: 'My father loved to sit here in the early evening. He was attracted to enclosed spaces with no windows.' I replied that I, too, was drawn to enclosed spaces, that retained a hint of winter even in midsummer. 'In that case,' said Yardena, 'I've brought you to the right place.'

5

FROM THE passage a creaking door gave access to a little room, simply furnished with a thread-bare sofa, a brown armchair and a brown coffee table with curved legs. On the wall hung a large, grey photograph of Tel Ilan, apparently taken many years ago from the top of the water tower in the middle of the village. Beside it I could see a framed certificate, but the light was too poor for me to read what it said. Yardena suggested we sit here for a bit, and I did not refuse. I sat down on the shabby sofa and Yardena sat facing me in the armchair. She crossed her legs and pulled her dress down, but it was too short to cover her knees. She said that we hadn't seen more than a small part of the house so far. The door on the left, she added, would take us back into the sitting room from which we had started our tour, while the one on the right led to the kitchen, from which we could go either to the pantry or to a corridor that led to a number of bedrooms. There were more bedrooms in another wing. There were bedrooms that no one had slept in for upwards of fifty years. Her great-grandfather sometimes used to put up visitors from remote settlements who came to look at his orchards and gardens. Her grand-father used to put up visiting lecturers and performers. I eyed her round knees that just peeped out from under her dress. Yardena looked at her knees too.

I hastened to divert my gaze and looked up at her face, which wore a faint, vague smile.

I asked her why she had taken me on this tour of the house. With an air of surprise she replied: 'I thought you wanted to buy it?' I was on the point of answering that I wanted to buy the house in order to demolish it, so there was no point in a lengthy visit, but on second thoughts I held my tongue. I said: 'It's such a big house for two women to live in alone.' Yardena said that her mother and grandmother lived in another part of the house that looked out onto the garden at the rear, and that she too had a little room there where she slept when she came to stay. 'Are you ready to press on now? You're not too tired? There are lots more rooms, and since you're here I'd like to take the opportunity to look at them myself. I'd be scared to go on my own, but the two of us together won't be scared, will we?'

There was hint of defiance, almost of sarcasm, in her voice as she asked if I was tired and if the two of us together would be scared. We went through the door on the right into a large, old-fashioned kitchen. A collection of different-sized pans hung from one wall, while an entire corner was taken up with an old kitchen range and a red-brick chimney. Bunches of garlic and strings of dried fruit were suspended from the ceiling. On a dark, rough-hewn table were scattered various utensils, notebooks, jars of ground spices, sardine tins, a dusty bottle of oil, a large knife, some old nuts, and various spreads and condiments. An illustrated calendar hanging on the wall was clearly many years old.

'My father used to love sitting here on winter days next to the hot kitchen range, writing in his notebooks,' Yardena said. 'Now my mother and my grandmother use a little kitchenette in their wing. This one is not really used.' She asked me if I was hungry and offered to put together a snack for me. I did actually feel quite peckish, and would happily have eaten, say, a slice of bread spread with avocado, with some onion and salt on top, but the kitchen seemed so bleak, and my curiosity spurred me onwards, deeper into the house, to the heart of the labyrinth. 'No, thanks, maybe some other time,' I said. 'Why don't we press on and see what else there is.'

Again I caught a hint of sardonic mockery in her eyes, as though she had plumbed the depths of my mind and discovered something that was not to my credit. 'Come on, this way,' she said. We took a narrow passage that led diagonally to the left into another, curved, passageway, where Yardena lit a pale light. My head was foggy and I wasn't certain I could find my own way back. Yardena seemed to enjoy leading me deeper and deeper into the bowels of the house, her bare feet still moving nimbly over the cold flagstones, her long, thin body dancing as she floated along. In this passageway various items of camping equipment were stowed away: a folded tent, poles, rubber mats, ropes, and a pair of sooty paraffin lamps. As if someone had been making preparations to go off and live alone in the mountains. An odour of dampness and dust hung between the thick walls. Once when I was eight or nine my father shut me up in the toolshed in the garden for an hour or two because I broke a thermometer. I can still remember the fingers of cold and darkness groping at me as I huddled like a foetus in a corner of the shed.

The curved passageway had three closed doors apart from the one we had come through. Indicating one of them, Yardena said that it led down into the cellar and asked me if I wanted to go down and see it.

'You're not scared of cellars, are you?'

'No, I'm not, but if you don't mind, maybe we'll skip the cellar this time.'

At once I had second thoughts, and said: 'Actually, why not? I ought to take a look at the cellar, too.'

Yardena reached for an electric torch hanging on the wall of the passage and pushed the door open with her bare foot. I followed, and in the semi-darkness, amid capering shadows, I counted fourteen steps. The air in the cellar was chilly and damp, and Yardena's torch cast heavy shadows on the dark walls. 'This is our cellar,' said Yardena. 'This is where we keep everything that there's no room for in the house. My father used to come down here sometimes on hot days like today to cool off. My grandfather used to sleep here, surrounded by barrels and packing cases, when the weather was really hot. You're not claustrophobic, are you? Are you scared of the dark? I'm not. On the contrary. Ever since I was a small girl, I have always found enclosed, dark hiding places for myself. If you do buy the house, try to persuade your clients not to make any drastic changes. At least while my grandmother is alive.'

'Changes? The new owners may not want to

change the house, they may want to knock it down and build a modern villa in its place.' (Something stopped me saying that I was planning to demolish it myself.)

'If only I had the money,' Yardena said, 'I'd buy it myself. Then I'd shut it up. I certainly wouldn't come and live here. I'd buy it and shut it up and let it stay this way. That's what I'd do.'

As my eyes grew accustomed to the dark I could see that the walls of the cellar were lined with shelves full of tins and jars, of pickled gherkins, olives, jams, various sorts of preserves, and other comestibles that I couldn't identify. It was as if the house were planning to withstand a lengthy siege. The floor was covered in heaps of sacks and boxes. To my right there were three or four sealed barrels that may have contained wine: I had no means of knowing. In one corner, books were piled one on top of another from the floor almost to the ceiling. According to Yardena, it was her great-grandfather, Gedalya Rubin, who had dug out and made this cellar, even before he built the house. The cellar was part of the foundations, and in the early years the family had lived here until the house itself was built above it. And then, as she'd told me earlier, the house wasn't built all at once; it had taken many years, with each generation adding its wings and extensions, which might be why it looked as though it had no plan. It was this muddle, Yardena said, that was for her one of the secret charms of the house: you could get lost, you could hide, and in moments of despair you could always find a quiet corner to be alone. 'Do you like being alone?' she asked.

I was surprised, because I couldn't imagine how anyone could need a quiet corner to be alone in in such a huge, rambling house, which was inhabited just by two old women, or sometimes by two old women and a barefoot student. Still, I felt good in the cellar. Its cool darkness was connected in my mind with the strange figure of that woman traveller who had appeared and promptly disappeared in the dusty, little garden behind the Village Hall, and with Benny Avni's odd invitation, and the heavy parcel I had found on a bench and had neglected to report to someone as I should have done.

I asked Yardena if there were a way of getting straight out of the cellar into the garden, but she told me there were only two ways out, the way we had come in or by some steps that led straight up into the living room. Did I want to go back? I said yes, but instantly regretted it, and said that, actually, no, I didn't. Yardena took my hand and sat me down on a packing case, then sat down opposite me, smoothing her dress over her crossed legs. 'Now,' she said, 'you and I aren't in a hurry to go anywhere, are we? Why don't you tell me what's really going to happen to our house once you've bought it.'

6

SHE PUT the torch down with its beam pointing up at the ceiling. A circle of light appeared on the ceiling, and the rest of the cellar was in darkness. Yardena became a silhouette among the shadows. 'If I wanted to,' she said, 'I could switch off the torch and slip away in the darkness; I could lock you in the cellar and you'd stay here for ever, eating olives and sauerkraut and drinking wine and groping at the walls till the battery runs out.' I wanted to reply that in my dreams I'd always seen myself locked in a dark cellar, but I chose to say nothing.

After a silence Yardena asked me who I would sell the house to. Who would buy an old warren like this?

'Let's see,' I said. 'Maybe I shan't sell it at all, maybe I'll move in here. I like the house. And the tenant, too. Maybe I'll buy the house with a sitting tenant?'

'I sometimes like to undress slowly in front of the mirror,' she said, 'imagining I'm a voracious man watching me undress. Games like that excite me.' The torchlight flickered for a moment as though the battery were low, but then the circle of bright light on the ceiling came back. In the silence I thought I could hear a vague sound of running water, water flowing slowly, quietly in some lower cellar underneath this one. When I was five or six my parents took me on a trip, to Galilee I suppose, and I dimly remember a building made of heavy, moss-covered stones, perhaps an ancient ruin, where you could also hear a distant sigh of water flowing in the darkness. I stood up and asked Yardena if there were other parts of the house that she wanted to show me. She aimed the beam of light at my face, so that I was dazzled, and asked mockingly why I was in such a hurry.

'The thing is,' I said, 'I don't want to take up your whole evening. And I've got to finish my income tax return this evening, too. And I've left my mobile phone on my desk, and Etty may be trying to get hold of me. And I'm going to have to come back anyway to talk to your mother and maybe your grandmother. But no, you're right, I'm not really in a hurry.'

She stopped dazzling me and pointed the torch at the floor between us. 'I'm not in a hurry, either,' she said. 'We've got the whole evening ahead of us, and the night is still young. Tell me a little bit about yourself. No, don't actually. I already know what I need to know, and whatever I don't know I don't need to know. My father used to lock me in this cellar for an hour or two when I was little whenever I annoyed him. For instance, once when I was eight or nine I was standing by his desk and I saw his manuscript full of heavy crossings out, so I picked up a pencil and drew a little cat smiling or a little monkey pulling faces on every page. I wanted to make him happy. But my father was furious and locked me in the cellar in the dark to teach me that I mustn't touch his papers, that I mustn't even look at them. I stayed here for a thousand years until he

153

sent my grandmother to let me out. And it worked:
I have never read any of his books and, when he
died, my grandmother, my mother and I sent all
his notebooks and his index cards and little slips to
the archive of the Writers' Union. We didn't want
to have to deal with his literary estate, Grandma
because she couldn't bear to read about the Holocaust,
it gave her nightmares, my mother because she
was angry with my father, and me for no particular
reason. I simply don't like his sort of books and I
can't stand the style. Once, in the sixth form, they
made us learn a chapter from one of his novels by
heart, and I felt, how can I put it, like he was impris-
oning and stifling me under his heavy winter blanket
with his body smells without any light or air. Since
then I have never read or even tried to read anything
he has written. How about you?'

I told her that I once tried to read one of Eldad
Rubin's novels, after all he was from here, from our
village, and the entire village was proud of him, but
I couldn't finish it; I read thrillers, agricultural supplements in the papers, and occasionally books about
politics or biographies of political leaders.

Yardena said: 'It's nice that you came tonight,

154

Yossi.' I reached out hesitantly and touched her shoulder, and when she didn't say anything I held her hand, and after a moment I took her other hand too, and so we sat for a few minutes face to face on two packing cases in the cellar, her hands clasped in mine as though the fact that neither of us had read any of Eldad Rubin's books forged a bond between us. Or maybe it wasn't that but the emptiness of the house and the silence of the cellar with its thick smells.

After a while, Yardena stood up. So did I. She withdrew her hands and held me tight, with all the warmth of her body, and I plunged my face into her long, brown hair and inhaled her smell, a smell of lemon-scented shampoo with a faint tinge of soap. And I kissed her twice, in the corners of her eyes. We stood there without moving, and I felt a strange mixture of desire and brotherly affection. 'Let's go to the kitchen and get something to eat,' she said, but she went on hugging me as though her body couldn't hear what her lips were saying to me. My hands stroked her back and her hands held my back tight and I could feel her breasts pressed to my chest and the feeling of brotherliness was still stronger than the desire. So I stroked her hair long and slow and I kissed the corners of her eyes again, but I avoided her lips, fearing to give up something irreplaceable. She buried her head in the hollow of my neck and the warmth of her skin radiated into my skin and stirred a silent joy that overcame the desire and reined in my body. Nor was her embrace one of desire but rather of wanting to hold onto me so that we shouldn't stumble.

7

A ND THEN in a corner of the cellar we discovered her father's old wheelchair, padded with worn out cushions and equipped with two big wheels each with a rubber hoop attached round it. Yardena sat me in the chair and started to push me to and fro across the cellar, from the steps to the heaps of sacks and from the shelves of preserved vegetables to the piled-up books. As she pushed me, she laughed, and said, 'Now I can do anything I feel like to you.' I laughed too, and asked what she felt like doing. She said she felt like putting me to sleep, into a sweet

cellar sleep. 'Go to sleep,' she said; 'sleep sweetly.'
There was something bittersweet in her voice as she
pronounced the short word. Then she began to sing
an old lullaby that I hadn't heard since my childhood, a strange, absurd song about shooting in the
night, about a father who is being shot at and a
mother who is soon going to take her turn on guard
duty: *The barn in Tel Yosef is burning, close your
eyes and do not weep, And from Beit Alfa smoke
is rising, close your eyes and go to sleep.*

The song somehow suited the house we were
in, and it specially suited the cellar and Yardena,
who kept on pushing me gently all round the cellar,
occasionally stroking my head and my face and softly
touching my lips till I really did begin to feel a pleasant
tiredness spreading through my body and I nearly
closed my eyes, except that some sense of danger
pierced the drowsiness and stopped me falling asleep.
My chin fell onto my chest and my mind wandered
to that strange woman who had appeared to me
beside the statue in the out-of-the-way Memorial
Garden behind the Village Hall, with her Alpine hiking
outfit and her hat with its buckles and brooches,
and I recalled how she had fixed me with a scornful

gaze and then, as I had walked away and turned my head, suddenly faded as if she had never existed. I would buy this house whatever the price, I decided, swathed in sweet sleepiness, and I would raze it to the ground though I had grown fond of it. Somehow I felt a certainty that the house had to be demolished, even if it was virtually the last one, and soon there would be no building left standing in Tel Ilan from the days of the first settlers. Barefoot Yardena kissed me on my head and left me in the wheelchair as she tiptoed away like a dancer and went up the steps with the torch and closed the door behind her, leaving me there in the wheelchair, sunk in a deep repose. And I knew that everything was all right and there was no hurry.

Waiting

1

T EL ILAN, a pioneer village, already a century old, was surrounded by fields and orchards. Vineyards sprawled down the east-facing slopes. Almond trees lined the approach road. Tiled roofs bathed in the thick greenery of ancient trees. Many of the inhabitants still farmed, with the help of foreign labourers who lived in huts in the farm-yards. But some had leased out their land and made a living by letting rooms, by running art galleries or fashion boutiques, or by working outside the village. Two gourmet restaurants had opened in the middle of the village, and there was also the winery and a shop selling tropical fish. One local entrepreneur had started manufacturing reproduction antique furniture. At weekends, of course, the village filled with visitors who came to eat or to hunt for a bargain. But every Friday afternoon its streets emptied as the residents rested behind closed shutters.

Benny Avni, the village Mayor, was a tall, thin, sloppily dressed man with drooping shoulders. His habit of wearing a pullover that was too big for him lent him an oafish air. He had a determined way of walking, his body bent forward as though he were walking into a wind. His face was pleasant, with a high brow, delicate lips, and an attentive, curious look in his brown eyes, as if to say: 'I like you, and I wish you'd tell me more about yourself.' Yet he also had the knack of refusing a request without appearing to do so.

At one o'clock one Friday afternoon in February Benny Avni was sitting alone in his office, replying to letters from local residents. All the council workers had already gone home, because on Fridays the offices closed at twelve. It was Benny Avni's custom to stay on late on Fridays to write personal replies to letters he had received. He had only a couple more letters to write, and then he was planning to go home, have his lunch, shower and take a siesta. Later he and his wife, Nava, were invited to a communal singing evening at the home of Dalia and Avraham Levin at the end of Pumphouse Rise.

He was still writing when he heard a timid knock

162

at the door. He was occupying a temporary office, furnished only with a desk, two chairs and a filing cabinet, while the council offices were undergoing refurbishment. 'Come in,' he said, looking up from his papers. A young Arab by the name of Adel entered. He was a student or an ex-student, who worked for Rachel Franco and lived in a shed at the bottom of her garden, at the edge of the village, near the row of cypress trees that marked the boundary of the cemetery. Benny knew him. He gave him a warm smile and told him to sit down.

Adel, short and skinny with glasses, remained standing facing the Mayor's desk, a couple of paces away from it. He bowed his head respectfully and apologised for disturbing him out of hours.

'Never mind, sit down,' said Benny Avni.

Adel hesitated, then sat down on the edge of the chair.

'It's like this,' he said. 'Your wife saw me walking towards the village centre and asked me to look in here and give you this: a letter, in fact.'

Benny Avni reached out and took the note.

'Where did you meet her?'

'Near the Memorial Garden.'

'Which way was she going?'

'She wasn't going anywhere. She was sitting on a bench.'

Adel stood up hesitantly, and asked if there was anything else the Mayor needed him for. Benny Avni smiled and shrugged, and said there was nothing he needed. Adel thanked him and left, with drooping shoulders. Not till he had gone did Benny Avni open up the folded note and find, in Nava's unhurried round handwriting, on a page torn from the notepad in the kitchen, the four words:

Don't worry about me.

He found these words puzzling. Every day Nava waited for him at home for lunch. He came home at one, whereas she finished working at the primary school at twelve. After seventeen years of marriage Nava and Benny still loved each other, but their everyday relations were marked most of the time by a measure of mutual indifference tinged with a certain contained impatience. She resented his political activities and his council work, which followed him home, and she could not stand the democratic affability that he lavished indiscriminately on everyone and anyone. For his part, he disliked her passion

164

for art, and the statuettes that she modelled in clay and fired in a special kiln. He hated the smell of burnt clay that sometimes clung to her clothes.

Benny Avni rang home and let the phone ring eight or nine times before admitting to himself that Nava was not there. He found it odd that she should go out at lunchtime, and even odder that she should send him a note, without bothering to say where she had gone or when she would be back. He found the note implausible, and her choice of messenger surprising. But he was not anxious. Nava and he always left each other notes under the vase in the living room if they went out unexpectedly.

So he finished off his last two letters, to Ada Dvash about relocating the post office and to the Council Treasurer about the pension rights of an employee, filed the contents of his in-tray, placed all his letters in the out-tray, checked the windows and shutters, put on his three-quarter-length suede coat, and double-locked the door. He planned to walk past the Memorial Garden, collect his wife from the bench where she was probably still sitting, and go home with her for lunch. He turned round, though, and went back to his office, because he had a feeling he might have forgotten to shut down the computer, or left a light on in the toilet. But the computer was shut down and the lights were all switched off, so Benny Avni double-locked his door again, and went off to look for his wife.

2

NAVA WAS not sitting on the bench by the Memorial Garden. In fact she was nowhere to be seen. But Adel, the skinny student, was sitting there, on his own, with an open book lying face down on his lap. He was staring at the street, while the sparrows chirruped overhead in the trees. Benny Avni laid his hand on Adel's shoulder:

'Has my wife been here?' he enquired gently, as if he feared he might hurt the boy. Adel replied that she had been there, but that she wasn't there any more.

'I can see that,' Benny Avni said, 'but I thought you might know which way she went.'

'I'm sorry,' said Adel. 'I'm really sorry.'

'That's all right,' said Benny Avni. 'It's not your fault.'

He made his way home, via Synagogue Street and Tribes of Israel Street. He leant forward as he walked, as though contending with some invisible obstacle. Everyone he passed greeted him with a smile, because the Mayor was a popular figure. He too smiled, and asked how they were, and what was new, and sometimes he added that the problem of the cracked paving stones was being taken care of. Soon they would all go home for their lunch and their Friday siesta, and the streets of the village would be empty.

The front door was unlocked, and the radio was playing softly in the kitchen. Someone was talking about the development of the railway network, and the advantages of rail over road transport. Benny Avni looked for a note from Nava in the usual place, under the vase in the living room, but there was none. His lunch was waiting for him, though, on the kitchen table, on a plate covered with another plate to keep it warm: a quarter of a chicken, with potato purée, carrots and peas. The plate was flanked by a knife and fork, and there was a folded napkin under the knife. Benny Avni put the plate in the microwave for two minutes, as, despite being covered, the food was not very warm. Meanwhile, he took a bottle of beer from the fridge and poured himself a glass. He consumed his lunch hungrily yet barely noticed what he ate, because he was listening to the radio, which was now broadcasting light music, with long breaks for commercials. During one of these breaks he thought he heard Nava's footsteps outside, on the garden path. He stared out of the kitchen window, but no one was there. Among the weeds and junk was the shaft of a broken cart, and a couple of rusty bicycles.

When he had finished eating, he put the dirty dishes in the sink and went to have a shower, turning off the radio on the way. A deep silence fell on the house. The only sound was the ticking of the clock on the wall. The twelve-year-old twin girls, Yuval and Inbal, were away on a school trip to Upper Galilee. The door to their bedroom was closed, and as he went past he opened it and peered inside. The shutters were closed, and there was a smell of soap and freshly ironed linen. Gently closing the door he went to the bathroom. After removing his shirt and trousers he suddenly recovered his presence of mind, and went to the telephone. He was still not worried, but he wondered where Nava had disappeared to and why she had not waited for him, as she always did, for lunch. He rang Gili Steiner, and asked if by any chance Nava was with her.

'No, she's not,' Gili said. 'Why? Did she tell you she was coming to see me?'

'That's just it, she didn't say anything.'

'The grocer is open till two, maybe she popped out to buy something.'

'Thanks, Gili. It's OK, she'll probably be back soon. I'm not worried.'

Despite which, he looked up the number of Victor's Grocery and dialled it. The phone rang for a long time before anyone answered. Eventually Old Liebersohn's nasal tenor voice spoke, in a liturgical singsong:

'Victor's Grocery, this is Shlomo Liebersohn speaking, how may I help you?'

Benny Avni asked after Nava, and Old Liebersohn replied mournfully:

'No, Comrade Avni, I am very sorry to say your lovely wife has not been seen here today. We have not had the pleasure of her charming company. Nor are we likely to, seeing that in ten minutes' time we are closing the shop and going home to prepare to welcome the Sabbath Bride.'

Benny Avni went to the bathroom, stripped off his underwear, adjusted the temperature of the water, and took a long shower. While he was drying himself he thought he heard the door creaking, so he called out 'Nava?', but there was no reply. Putting on clean underwear and a pair of khaki trousers he combed the kitchen for clues, then went to the living room and checked the corner where the TV was. He looked in their bedroom and in the enclosed veranda which served as Nava's studio. This was where she spent long hours modelling figurines in clay, imaginary creatures, or boxers with square jaws and broken noses. She baked them in a kiln in the storage shed. He went to the shed, switched on the light and stood there blinking for a moment, but all he could see were the contorted figures, and the cold kiln surrounded by dark shadows cavorting among the dusty shelves.

Benny Avni wondered if he should go and lie down without waiting for her. He went to the kitchen, and putting his dirty dishes in the dishwasher, he looked for clues as to whether Nava had eaten before going out, but the dishwasher was almost full, and he could not identify which plates, if any, Nava had used for her lunch.

There was a saucepan on the stove with some cooked chicken in it, but it was impossible to tell whether Nava had eaten or not. Benny Avni sat down by the phone and rang Batya Rubin's number, to see if Nava was with her, but the phone rang and rang and no one answered. 'Really,' Benny said to himself, and went to the bedroom to lie down. Nava's slippers were by the bed. They were small, brightly coloured, and rather worn at the heel; they looked like a pair of toy boats. He lay on his back for a quarter of an hour or twenty minutes, staring at the ceiling. Nava took offence easily, and he had learnt over the years that any attempt to mollify her only upset her more, so he preferred to say nothing and allow the passage of time to soothe her. She contained herself, but she never forgot. Once her friend Gili Steiner, the doctor, had suggested holding a little exhibition of Nava's figurines in the council art gallery. Benny Avni had promised with a smile that he would think about it and let Gili know. In the end he had decided that it would not be proper to hold the exhibition in the council's gallery: after all, Nava was only an amateur artist, and she could display her work in a corridor at the school where she worked, so as to avoid imputations of favouritism, and so on. Nava had said nothing, but for several nights she stood ironing in their bedroom till three or four in the morning. She had ironed everything, even the towels and bedspreads.

After twenty minutes or so Benny Avni suddenly got up, dressed, went down to the cellar, switched on the light, unleashing a swarm of insects, peered at the packing cases and suitcases, fingered the power drill, tapped the wine barrel, which responded with a hollow sound, turned off the light, went upstairs to the kitchen, hesitated for a moment or two, put on his three-quarter-length suede coat over his shapeless pullover, and left the house without locking up. Leaning forward as though contending with a strong headwind, he went in search of his wife.

3

ON FRIDAY afternoons there was never anybody about in the village. Everyone was at home, resting in preparation for going out in the evening. It was a grey, humid day. Clouds hung low over the rooftops, and skeins of fine mist drifted in the streets, lined with shuttered, slumbering houses. A scrap of old newspaper fluttered across the empty street: Benny stooped, picked it up, and put it in a rubbish bin. A big mongrel approached him near the Pioneers' Garden and started to follow him, growling and baring its teeth. Benny shouted at the dog, but it became angry and seemed likely to leap at him. Benny stooped, picked up a stone, and waved his arm in the air. The dog continued to follow him at a safe distance, its tail between its legs. So they both proceeded along the empty street, some thirty feet apart, and turned left into Founders' Street. Here too all the shutters were closed for the siesta. They were mostly old wooden shutters painted a faded green. Some of the slats were bent or missing.

Here and there, in yards that had once been farmyards but were now uncared for, Benny Avni noticed a disused dovecote, a goat shed that had been converted into a storeroom, an abandoned truck overgrown with weeds near a corrugated-iron barn or a kennel no longer in use. Mighty palm trees grew in front of the houses. There had been two old palm trees in front of his house, but at Nava's request they had both been cut down four years previously, because the rustling of their fronds in the breeze outside their bedroom window had disturbed her sleep at night and made her feel irritable and sad.

Jasmine and asparagus fern grew in some gardens, whereas in others there was nothing but weeds, and tall pine trees whispering in the wind. Bent forward in his usual way, Benny Avni went along Founders' Street and Tribes of Israel Street, passed the Memorial Garden, and paused for a moment by the bench where, according to Adel, Nava had been sitting when she had asked him to take the note saying *'Don't worry about me'* to Benny in his temporary office.

The dog, too, paused, some thirty feet away from him. It was not growling or baring its teeth now, but staring at Benny Avni with an intelligent, inquisitive air. Nava and he had both been single and studying in Tel Aviv when she became pregnant. She was training to be a teacher and he was doing business studies. They had agreed at once that the unwanted pregnancy must be terminated, but two hours before the time of her appointment at a private clinic in Reines Street, Nava had changed her mind. Laying her head on his chest she had begun to cry.

He had refused to give in, though: he had pleaded with her to be reasonable, there was no alternative, and, after all, the whole thing was no worse than having a wisdom tooth removed.

He had waited for her in a café across the road from the clinic. He had read two newspapers; he even read the sports supplement. Nava had emerged after two hours, looking pale, and they had taken a taxi back to their room in a student residence. Six or seven noisy students were there, waiting for Benny Avni. They had come for some meeting that had been arranged long before. Nava got into the bed in the corner of the room and pulled the bedclothes over her head, but the arguments, the shouting, the jokes and the cigarette smoke permeated through to her nonetheless. She felt weak and nauseous. She groped her way through the assembled company, leaning on the wall for support, until she reached the toilet. Her head was going round and the pain was coming back as the effects of the anaesthetic wore off. In the toilet she found that someone had been sick all over the floor and the seat. Unable to stop herself, she threw up too. She stood there for a long time, crying, with her hands on the

175

wall and her head on her hands, until the noisy visitors had left and Benny found her, shivering. He put his arm round her shoulders and gently led her back to bed. They were married two years later, but Nava had trouble conceiving. Various doctors helped her with all sorts of treatments. It was another five years before the twin girls, Yuval and Inbal, were born. Nava and Benny never spoke about that afternoon in the student room in Tel Aviv. It was as if they had agreed that there was no need to talk about it. Nava taught at the school and in her spare time she modelled clay figures of monsters and broken-nosed boxers that she fired in a kiln in the store shed. Benny Avni was elected Mayor, and most of the villagers liked him because he was unassuming and a good listener, though he also had the knack of getting others to do what he wanted, without their noticing.

4

ON THE corner of Synagogue Street he stopped for a moment and turned to see if the dog was still following him. It was standing by a gate, with

its tail between its legs and mouth open, watching
Benny with patient curiosity. Benny called to it softly
and the dog pricked up its ears and let its pink
tongue loll out. It seemed to be interested in Benny,
but preferred to keep its distance. There was not
another living soul abroad, not even a cat or a bird,
just Benny and the mongrel, and the clouds that
had come down so low that they almost touched
the tops of the cypresses.

The water tower stood on three concrete legs, and
next to it there was an air-raid shelter. Benny Avni
tried the metal door and discovering that it was not
locked went inside and down the twelve steps. A damp,
stagnant draught touched his skin as he felt for the
light switch. There was no power. Even so, he entered
the dark space and groped among vaguely identifi-
able objects, a pile of mattresses or folding beds and
some kind of broken chest of drawers. He inhaled the
heavy air, and groped his way back through the darkness towards the steps, trying the light switch again
as he passed it. There was still no power. He closed
the iron door and returned to the empty street.

The wind had dropped, but the mist still billowed
and blurred the outlines of the old houses, some

of which were indeed more than a century old. The yellow plaster had cracked and crumbled on the walls, leaving dirty bald patches. Grey pines grew in the gardens, and the properties were divided from one another by hedges of cypress. Here and there a rusting lawnmower or a disintegrating washtub could be seen in a jungle of grass, nettles, couch grass and convolvulus.

Benny Avni whistled softly but the dog continued to keep its distance. In front of the synagogue, which had been erected when the village was founded, back at the beginning of the twentieth century, there was a noticeboard to which were pinned advertisements for the films showing at the local cinema and the products of the winery, as well as some council notices bearing his own signature. Benny paused for a moment to look at these notices, but for some reason they seemed to him redundant or totally erroneous. He thought he caught sight of a stooping figure at the corner of the street, but as he drew closer he saw only bushes in the mist. A metal menorah surmounted the synagogue, and lions and six-pointed stars of David were carved on the doors. He climbed the five steps and tried the door, which was not locked. It was almost dark inside the synagogue, and the air was chilly and dusty. A curtain hung in front of the ark, and the feeble light of the Eternal Lamp lit the words '*I have set the Lord always before me*'. Benny Avni wandered among the pews in the half-light, then went upstairs to the women's gallery. Black bound prayer books lay scattered on the benches. He was hit by a smell of old sweat, along with an odour of old books. He ran his hand over the back of a bench: it seemed as though someone had left a shawl or headscarf behind.

When he left the synagogue, Benny Avni found the dog waiting for him at the bottom of the steps. He stamped his foot and said, 'Shoo. Go away.' The dog, which wore a collar with an identification tag hanging from it, tipped its head a little to one side, opened its mouth and panted, as if waiting for an explanation. But no explanation was forthcoming. Benny turned to go on his way, his shoulders hunched and his shapeless pullover peeking out from under his three-quarter-length suede coat. He took big strides, his body inclined forward like the prow of a ship cleaving the waves. The dog did not abandon him, but still kept its distance.

Where could she have gone? Maybe she was visiting

one of her women friends and had lost track of the time. Maybe she had stayed on late at school because of some urgent matter. Maybe she was at the clinic. A few weeks previously, during a quarrel, she had told him that his friendliness was just a mask, behind which there was a frozen wasteland. He had not replied, but merely smiled affectionately, as he always did when she was angry with him. Nava was beside herself with rage. 'You don't care about anything, do you?' she said. 'Not me, and not the girls.' He had continued to smile affectionately and had put his hand on her shoulder, but she shook it off violently and left, slamming the door. An hour later he brought her a hot herb tea with honey in her studio. He thought she might be developing a cold. She wasn't, but she took the drink and said gently:

'Thank you. You really didn't have to.'

5

PERHAPS WHILE he was wandering the streets in the mist she was back at home? He considered for a moment whether to go home, but the thought of the empty house, and particularly the image of the empty bedroom with her colourful slippers like toy boats at the foot of the bed, deterred him and he decided to press on. With his shoulders inclined forward he walked along Vine Street and Tarpat Street until he reached the primary school where Nava worked. Only a month earlier he himself had battled with his opponents on the council and even with the Ministry of Education and had succeeded in obtaining funding for the construction of four new classrooms and a spacious gymnasium.

The iron gates of the school were locked for the weekend. The school building and the playground were surrounded by iron railings topped with coils of barbed wire. Benny Avni circled the site twice before he found a place where it was possible to climb into the playground. He waved to the dog, which was watching him from the other side of the road, took hold of the iron railings and hoisted his body up, pushed the barbed wire to one side, scratching himself in the process, and half-jumped, half-rolled into the playground, twisting his ankle as he landed. He limped across the playground, dripping blood from his lacerated left hand.

181

Entering the school building through a side door he found himself in a long corridor. Several classrooms opened off it on either side. There was a smell of sweat, food and chalk-dust. The floor was littered with scraps of paper and orange peel. He went into a classroom whose door was ajar and on the teacher's desk he found a dusty cloth and a piece of paper torn from an exercise book, on which a few lines were scribbled. He inspected the handwriting: it was indeed a woman's writing, but it was not Nava's. Benny Avni replaced the paper, which was now stained with his blood, on the desk and turned to look at the blackboard, on which was written in the same womanly hand: 'The calm of village life compared with the bustle of the town. Please finish by Wednesday at the latest.' Underneath appeared the words: 'Read the next three chapters carefully at home and prepare to answer the questions.' On the wall hung pictures of Theodor Herzl, of the President and the Prime Minister, as well as some posters illustrating slogans such as 'Nature lovers respect wild flowers.'

The benches were all higgledy-piggledy as if the pupils had been in so great a hurry to leave when the bell rang that they had simply pushed them aside. The geraniums in the window boxes looked sad and neglected. On the wall opposite the teacher's desk hung a large map of Israel with the village of Tel Ilan in the Manasseh Hills circled in green. A solitary pullover hung on the coathooks. Benny Avni left the classroom and limped around the deserted corridors. Drops of blood from his scratched hand marked his passage. When he reached the toilets at the end of the first corridor something drew him to the girls' toilets. He found the smell slightly different from that of boys' toilets. There were five cubicles, and Benny Avni checked to see what was behind each door. He even looked into the cleaning cupboard. Then he retraced his steps and took another corridor, and another, until he finally found the door to the teachers' common room. Here he paused for a moment, feeling the metal plate with the words 'Teachers' Common Room. No entry for pupils without special permission.' For a moment he had a feeling that some sort of meeting was going on behind the closed door, and he was afraid of disturbing it, yet also eager to interrupt. But the common room was empty, and dark, too, its curtains drawn over the closed windows.

Bookcases lined two walls of the room, and in the middle was a large table with a couple of dozen chairs. Empty and half-empty tea and coffee cups littered the table, together with books, timetables, printed circulars and notebooks. Next to the far window was a large cabinet with a drawer for each teacher. He found Nava Avni's drawer, pulled it out and laid it on the table. It contained a pile of exercise books, a box of chalks, a packet of throat pastilles and an old sunglasses case with nothing in it. After a moment's thought he put the drawer back in its place.

On the back of one of the chairs Benny Avni noticed a scarf that looked familiar. But it was too dark for him to be sure if it was one of Nava's. Still, he picked it up, wiped the blood off his hand, folded it and put it in the pocket of his suede coat. Then he left the common room and limped along one corridor with several doors opening off it, and then along another. On his way he peered into each classroom, tried the door of the nurse's room, which was locked, glanced into the janitor's room, and finally left the building through a different door from the one he had entered by. He limped across the playground, climbed the railings and pushed the barbed wire aside again, then jumped down into the street, this time ripping the sleeve of his coat.

He stood waiting for a moment, not knowing what he was really waiting for, until he caught sight of the dog sitting on the opposite pavement staring at him earnestly from a distance of some thirty feet. It occurred to him to try to get closer and stroke the dog, but it stood up, stretched, and walked slowly ahead, maintaining the established distance.

6

FOR A quarter of an hour or so he limped after the dog through the empty streets, his bleeding hand wrapped in the scarf he had taken from the common room, the check scarf that might have been Nava's or might simply have looked like one of hers. The low grey sky was tangled in the tops of the trees and banks of mist lay along the gardens. He thought he felt some fine drops of rain on his face, but he was not sure and he didn't care. He glanced at a low wall where he thought he saw a bird, but it turned out to be nothing more than an empty tin can.

He went down a narrow lane bordered with high bougainvillea hedges. He had recently approved the repaving of this lane and had even come along one morning to inspect the work. From the lane they turned into Synagogue Street again, the dog leading the way, and this time the light was greyer still. He wondered if he should go straight home: she might have returned by now, she might be lying down, wondering where he had gone, and perhaps even, who knew, worrying about him. But thinking about the empty house alarmed him and he continued to limp after the dog, which walked ahead of him without looking back, its muzzle held low as if sniffing the way. Soon, maybe before nightfall, heavy rain would fall, washing the dusty trees and all the roofs and pavements. He thought about what might have been and would now never come to pass, but his thoughts wandered. Nava used to like to sit with the two girls on the back veranda, which overlooked the lemon trees, chatting softly to them. What they talked about he had never known, and had never taken the trouble to find out. Now he wondered, but had no clue. He had the feeling that he must make a decision, but though he was used to making many decisions every day, this time he was beset with uncertainty; in fact he had no idea what was being asked of him. Meanwhile, the dog had stopped and sat down on the pavement thirty feet away from him, so he too stopped, in front of the Memorial Garden, and sat down on the bench where apparently his wife had been sitting two or three hours earlier when she asked Adel to look into his temporary office and give him her note. So he settled in the middle of the bench, his bleeding hand wrapped in the scarf, buttoned up his coat because of the light rain that had started to fall, and sat waiting for his wife.

Strangers

1

I T WAS evening. A bird called twice. What it meant there was no way of telling. A breeze stirred and stopped. Old folk brought chairs out and sat in their doorways watching the passers-by. From time to time a car went past and disappeared round the bend in the road. A woman walked by slowly, carrying a shopping basket, on her way home from the grocer's. A crowd of children filled the street with noise, which died down as they moved away. Behind the hill a dog barked, and another dog answered. The sky was turning grey, and the glow of sunset could only be seen to the west, through the shadowy cypresses. The mountains in the distance were black.

Kobi Ezra, an unhappy seventeen-year-old, stood waiting behind a eucalyptus tree whose trunk was painted white. He was thin and frail-looking, with skinny legs, swarthy skin, and a perpetual expression of sad wonderment, as if he had just had an unpleasant surprise. He was wearing dusty jeans and a T-shirt bearing the legend *Three Giants Festival*. He was desperately in love and confused: the woman he loved was almost twice his age, she already had a lover, and he suspected that all she felt for him was polite pity. He hoped that she would guess how he felt, but feared that if she did, she would reject him. This evening, if her boyfriend didn't come in his diesel tanker, he would offer to walk her from the post office, where she worked in the daytime, to the library, where she worked in the evenings. Maybe this time he would finally try to say something that would make her understand his feelings.

The postmistress, Ada Dvash, who was also the librarian, was a thirty-year-old divorcee. She was short, jolly, plump and smily. Her shoulder-length fair hair fell more on her left shoulder than on the right. Her large wooden earrings swayed as she walked. Her eyes were warm and brown, and a slight squint enhanced her charm, as though she squinted on purpose, mischievously. She enjoyed her work at the post office and at the library, which she carried out painstakingly and precisely. She loved summer fruit and was fond of light music. At seven-thirty every morning she sorted the incoming mail and put the letters and packets in the residents' boxes. At half past eight she opened the post office for business. At one o'clock she closed and went home to eat and rest, then opened again from five to seven. At seven she closed the post office, and twice a week, on Mondays and Wednesdays, she went straight off to open the library. She worked alone, handling packets, parcels, telegrams and registered letters, and offered a warm welcome to customers who came to buy stamps or aerogrammes, to pay their bills or fines, or to register the purchase or sale of a car. Everyone liked her easy manner, and if there was no queue at the single counter they lingered for a chat.

The village was so small that not many people came into the post office. Most simply checked their mail in the boxes that were fixed to the outside wall and went on their way. Sometimes an hour or an hour and a half went by without anyone coming inside. Ada Dvash sat at her counter sorting mail, filling in forms, or arranging packets in a precise rectangular pile. Sometimes, people said in the village,

193

she was visited by a man in his forties with bushy eyebrows joined in the middle, not from our village, a tall, heavily built man who always wore blue overalls and work boots. He parked his diesel tanker opposite the post office, and sat waiting for her on the bench in the entrance, amusing himself by throwing his bunch of keys in the air and catching it in one hand. Whenever his tanker was parked opposite the post office or in front of her house, people in the village said, 'Ada Dvash's boyfriend has come for another honeymoon.' This was not said maliciously but almost affectionately, because Ada Dvash was popular in the village. When her husband left her four years previously, most of the village sided with her rather than with him.

2

B Y THE last light of day the boy found a stick at the foot of the eucalyptus tree and he used it to scratch shapes of people in the dust while he waited for Ada Dvash to finish work at the post office. They came out distorted, as though his drawings were done out of loathing. But the light was fading, so no one could see them; in fact he could hardly see them himself. Then he scuffed them all out with his sandal, raising a cloud of dust. He tried to find suitable words to speak to Ada Dvash as he walked her from the post office to the library. On the two previous occasions when he had accompanied her, he spoke with such fervour of his love of books and music that he did not manage to communicate any real emotion. Maybe this time he should talk to her about loneliness? But she might form the impression that he was referring to her divorce, and she might be offended or hurt. The last time she had told him about her love for the Bible, and how she read a chapter every night before she went to sleep. So maybe this time he should start by talking about biblical love stories? About David, and his love for Saul's daughter Michal? Or about the Song of Songs? But his knowledge of the Bible was limited, and he was afraid that Ada might despise him if he started talking about a subject he did not understand. Better to talk to her about animals: he loved animals and felt an affinity with them. For example, he might talk about the mating habits of certain songbirds. Maybe he could use the songbirds to hint at his own feelings. But what chance did a seventeen-year-old boy have with a woman in her thirties? At best he might manage to stir a certain pity. And the distance from pity to love was like the distance from the moon reflected in a puddle to the moon itself.

Meanwhile, the light was fading. A few old folk were still sitting on their chairs in front of their doors, dozing or staring in front of them, but most had folded their chairs and gone indoors. The street was emptying. Jackals howled in the vineyards on the hills round the village, and the village dogs answered them with frenzied barking. A single, distant shot disturbed the darkness, followed by the sweeping torrent of the crickets' chirping. *Just a few more minutes and she'll come out, lock the post office, and set out for the library. You will appear out of the shadows and ask, like the two previous times, if you can walk with her.*

He had not yet finished reading the book that she lent him last time, *Mrs Dalloway*, but he wanted to ask her for another one, because he planned to spend the whole weekend reading. 'Haven't you got any friends? Don't you have plans to go out?' No, the plain truth was that he had no friends, and no plans. He preferred to stay in his room, reading or listening to music. His school friends enjoyed making a noise, being surrounded by noise, whereas he preferred silence. That's what he'd tell her this time. And she'd see for herself that he was different. Special. 'Why the hell do you always have to be different from everyone else?' his father kept saying to him. 'You should get out, do some sport.' His mother came into his room every evening to check if he had clean socks to put on. One evening he locked himself in. The next day his father confiscated the key.

He scratched at the whitewashed bark of the euca-lyptus with his stick, and then felt his chin to check how the shave administered two hours earlier was holding up. From his chin he passed his fingers over his cheek and forehead, imagining that his fingers were her fingers. The bus from Tel Aviv arrived shortly before seven and pulled up in front of the council offices. From his hiding place behind the eucalyptus Kobi saw people getting off carrying bags and packages. Among them he identified Dr Steiner

197

and also his teacher, Rachel Franco. They were talking about Rachel's old father, who had gone out to buy a newspaper and forgotten the way home. Their voices reached him, but he could not make out the thread of their conversation, nor did he want to. As the passengers dispersed their voices faded in the distance. And the crickets' chirping could be heard again.

Ada Dvash came out of the post office at seven precisely. She locked the door, locked the heavy padlock too, checked that it was properly fixed and crossed the empty street. She was wearing a loose-fitting summer blouse and a full, light skirt. Kobi Ezra emerged from his hiding place and said softly, as if afraid to startle her:

'It's me again. Kobi. May I walk with you?'

'Good evening,' said Ada Dvash. 'How long have you been standing here?'

Kobi was about to lie, but for some reason the truth came out instead:

'I've been waiting for you for half an hour. Even a bit more.'

'Why were you waiting for me?'

'No special reason.'

198

'You could have come straight to the library.'

'Sure. But I felt like waiting here.'

'Have you brought back a book?'

'I haven't finished it yet. I came to ask you to let me have another book for the weekend. I'll finish them both.' And so he started telling her, as they walked up Founders' Street, that he was almost the only boy in his class who read books. The rest were addicted to computers or sport. The girls, yes, a few, there were some girls who read. Ada Dvash knew this but did not want mention it, so as not to embarrass him. He walked along beside her, talking non-stop, as though he were scared that if he paused even for a moment she would be able to guess his secret. She guessed it anyway, and wondered how she could avoid hurting him while not giving him the wrong idea. She had to restrain herself forcibly from reaching out and stroking his hair, which was cut short apart from a little quiff that stuck up in front and gave him a childlike air.

'Haven't you got any friends?'

'The boys are childish, and the girls are not attracted to someone like me.'

Then he added suddenly:

199

'You're not exactly like the others, either.'

She smiled in the dark, and straightened the neck-line of her blouse, which was askew. Her big wooden earrings swayed when she walked as if they had a life of their own. Kobi went on talking non-stop. Now he was saying that society mistrusts and even despises people of true worth. As he talked he felt an urge to touch the woman who was walking beside him, however lightly or fleetingly. He reached out and nearly touched her shoulders with his finger-tips but at the last moment he drew back, clenched his fist and let his arm drop. Ada Dvash said:

'There's a dog in this yard that once chased me and bit my leg. Let's hurry past.'

When Ada mentioned her leg the boy blushed, glad that it was too dark for her to notice. But she did notice something: not his blushing but his sudden silence. Tenderly she touched his back and asked what he thought of *Mrs Dalloway*. Kobi started talking about the book excitedly, his voice unstable and strained, as though he were confessing his feelings. He spoke for a long time about *Mrs Dalloway* and other books, maintaining that life only has meaning if it is devoted to some idea or emotion round which everything revolves. Ada Dvash liked his elaborate diction but wondered if it was not one of the reasons he was so lonely and had apparently never had a girlfriend. He was still talking when they reached the library, which occupied the ground floor of the rear extension to the Village Hall. They went in by a side entrance. Since there was ten minutes to go before opening time, which was seven-thirty, Ada suggested making them both a cup of coffee. Kobi began by murmuring, 'No, thanks, there's no need, really,' but then he changed his mind and said, 'Actually, why not, yes please,' and asked if he could help.

3

THE LIBRARY was lit by bright, white neon lighting. Ada switched on the air conditioning, which started with a soft gurgling sound. The library consisted of a smallish space lined with white-painted metal bookcases, and off this three parallel aisles of shelves opened, lit slightly less glaringly by the neon lighting. Near the entrance there was a desk on which were a computer, a telephone, a pile of brochures and periodicals, two piles of books and an old radio.

She disappeared from view down one of the aisles, at the end of which there was a sink and the entrance to the toilet. There she filled the kettle and switched it on. While waiting for the water to boil she turned on the computer and sat Kobi next to her behind the desk. Looking down he observed that her lemon-coloured skirt ended above her knees. His face turned red again at the sight of her knees, and he laid his arms on his lap, then thought better of it and crossed them on his chest, and finally placed his hands on the desk. As she looked at him, he thought the slight squint in her left eye was giving him a wink, as though to say, 'It's not so bad, Kobi. So, you're blushing again.'

The water boiled. Ada Dvash made two cups of black coffee and put sugar in without asking him. She pushed one cup towards him. She looked at his T-shirt with the words *Three Giants Festival* and wondered what sort of festival it was, and who the Three Giants were. It was twenty to eight, and no one had come into the library. At one end of the desk was a pile of five or six new books that had been acquired during the previous week. Ada showed Kobi how new acquisitions are catalogued on the computer, how the books are stamped with the library's stamp, how they are covered with strong plastic film, and how a label showing the number is stuck on the spine of the book.

'From now on you're the Assistant Librarian,' she said, adding, 'Tell me, aren't you expected at home? For supper? They might be worried about you.' The squint in her left eye winked affectionately.

'You haven't had supper either.'

'But I always eat after I've closed the library. I grab something from the fridge and eat it in front of the TV.'

'I'll walk you home when you've finished. So you don't have to walk alone in the dark.'

She smiled at him and laid her warm hand on his:

'There's no need, Kobi. I only live five minutes away.'

At the touch of her hand a sweet shiver ran from the back of his neck to the base of his spine. But he inferred from her words that her boyfriend, the one who drove a diesel tanker, must be waiting for her at home. And even if he wasn't there already, she might be expecting him later in the evening. That was why she had said there was no need for him to walk her home. But he would follow her anyway, like a dog, to the doorstep of her house, and when she closed the door he'd stay, sitting on the steps. This time he would also shake her hand to say goodnight, and when her hand was inside his he'd squeeze it lightly twice, so that she'd understand. There was something wrong, twisted and despicable about a world where a diesel tanker driver has more advantages than you just because he's older. He could suddenly see the tanker driver in his mind's eye, with his thick eyebrows joined in the middle, inserting his fat fingers into the front of her blouse. This apparition made him feel lust and shame together with a desperate anger and a desire to do something to hurt her.

Ada looked at him out of the corner of her eye and noticed something. She suggested they take a look around the shelves: she could show him all sorts of minor treasures, such as the writings of Eldad Rubin with corrections in his own handwriting in the margins. But, before he could answer, two older women came in, one small and square-shaped, with baggy three-quarter-length shorts and dyed red hair, the other with short, grey hair and protruding eyes behind thick glasses. They had brought their books back and wanted to borrow some new ones. They chatted to each other and to Ada about a new Israeli novel that the whole country was talking about. Kobi escaped down one of the aisles where, on a low shelf, he came across Virginia Woolf's *To the Lighthouse*. He stood and read a couple of pages so as not to have to listen to the conversation. But the women's voices broke in on him and he found himself overhearing what they were saying.

'If you want to know what I think,' one of them was saying, 'he keeps repeating himself. He writes the same book over and over again with small changes.'

'Dostoevsky and Kafka also repeat themselves,' her friend said. 'So what?'

Ada remarked with a smile: 'There are some subjects and motifs that a writer comes back to again and again because apparently they come from the root of his being.'

When Ada said the words 'the root of his being' Kobi felt something squeezing at his heart. At that moment it was clear to him that she had meant him to overhear the phrase, that she had been talking to him rather than to the women, and that she had been trying to say that both their innermost souls shared a single root. In his imagination he approached her, putting his arm round her shoulders, and resting her head on his shoulder because he was a full head taller than she was. He could feel her breasts pressed against his chest, her stomach against his stomach, and then the image became so piercing that it was unbearable.

He stayed where he was for a moment or two after the women left, while his body calmed down, and said to Ada in a voice slightly deeper than usual that he would be with her in a moment. Meanwhile, she entered in the computer the books that the two women had returned and had borrowed.

Ada Dvash and Kobi sat side by side at the desk, as if he too were working in the library. The silence between them was broken only by the humming of the air conditioning and the buzzing of the neon light. They talked about Virginia Woolf, who had drowned herself at the height of the Second World War. Ada said she could not understand how anyone

could commit suicide in the midst of a war. It was
hard to imagine that she hadn't had an iota of a
sense of involvement, or any curiosity to know how
things would turn out, and which side would be
victorious in that terrible war that would affect
everybody in the world in one way or another. Didn't
she even want to know whether her own country,
England, would survive or would be conquered by
the Nazis?

'She was in despair,' Kobi said.

'That's just what I don't understand,' Ada said.
'There's always at least one thing that is precious
to you and that you don't want to be parted from.
Even just a cat or a dog. Or your favourite armchair.
The view of the garden in the rain. Or the sunset
from the window.'

'You're a happy person. Despair is obviously alien
to you.'

'No, not alien. But it doesn't attract me either.'

A bespectacled girl in her twenties came into the
library. She had full hips and was wearing a flowery
blouse and tight-fitting jeans. She screwed up her
eyes at the bright neon light, smiled at Ada and at
Kobi, asked Kobi if he was going to be the deputy

librarian. She wanted some help looking for material on the events of 1936–39, otherwise known as the Arab Revolt. Ada showed her sections on the history of Israel and the Middle East, and the two of them pulled out one book after another and examined the tables of contents.

Kobi went to the sink next to the toilet and washed the two coffee cups. The clock above the desk showed twenty to nine. *Another evening will go by without you revealing your feelings. This time you mustn't let the chance slip. When you're both alone again you must take her hand in your hands and look her straight in the eyes and tell her at last. But what are you going to tell her? And what if she bursts out laughing? Or if she panics and pulls her hand away? Or she might be sorry for you and press your head to her chest and stroke your hair. Like a child.* Pity seemed to him more terrifying than any rejection. It was clear to him that if she behaved as if she were sorry for him he would not be able to stop himself from bursting out crying. There was no way he could hold back his tears. And then it would all be over, and he would run away from her into the darkness.

Meanwhile, even though the coffee cups were dry he kept on rubbing them with the tea towel that hung on a hook next to the sink, staring as he did so at a moth that was hurling itself desperately at the neon tube.

4

THE BESPECTACLED woman said thank you and left, carrying five or six books on the Arab Revolt in a plastic bag. Ada entered the details of the books on the computer from the cards that lay in front of her on the desk. She explained to Kobi that she was not really allowed to lend more than two books at a time, but that this girl had to hand in an essay in ten days' time.

'It'll be nine o'clock soon, and then we'll shut the library and go home,' she said.

At the sound of the words 'go home' Kobi's heart started to pound in his chest as though they contained some secret promise. The next moment he crossed his legs because his body was aroused again and threatened to embarrass him. An inner voice said to him that come shame or mockery or pity he mustn't give up, he had to tell her.

'Ada, listen.'

'Yes.'

'Do you mind if I ask you something personal?'

'Go on.'

'Have you ever loved someone with no hope that he will return your love?'

She saw at once where he was leading, and hesitated for a moment between her affection for the boy and her duty to be very careful with his feelings. And underneath these two she also felt a vague impulse to accede.

'Yes, but it was a long time ago.'

'What did you do?'

'What all girls do. I stopped eating, cried at night, started by wearing pretty, attractive clothes and then deliberately dressed drably. Until it passed. It does pass, Kobi, even though at the time it seems that it'll last for ever.'

'But I –'

Another reader came in. This time it was a woman in her mid-seventies, shrivelled and brisk, dressed in a light summer dress that was much too young for her, with silver bracelets on her skinny, tanned arms and a double row of amber beads round her neck. She greeted Ada and asked inquisitively:

'And who is this charming young man? Where did you find him?'

With a smile Ada said:

'This is my new assistant.'

'I know you,' the old woman said, turning to Kobi, 'you're Victor Ezra the grocer's son. Are you a volunteer?'

'Yes, no, that is –'

'He's come to help me,' Ada said. 'He loves books.'

The woman returned a novel in a foreign language and asked if she could borrow the book by the Israeli writer that everyone was talking about, the one that the two women who had come earlier had requested. Ada said there was a long waiting list, as there were only two copies in the library.

'Shall I put you on the list, Lisa? It'll take between a month and two months.'

'Two months?' the woman said. 'In that time he'll have written another book.'

Ada persuaded her to make do with a novel

211

translated from Spanish that had had good reviews, and the woman left.

'What an unpleasant woman,' Kobi said. 'And she's a gossip, too.'

Ada did not reply. She was leafing through the book the woman had returned. Kobi felt a sudden sense of urgency that was almost more than he could bear. Here they were alone again, but in another ten minutes' time she would say that it was closing time and the moment would be lost, this time perhaps for ever. He suddenly hated the blinding white neon light, like at the dentist's, which seemed to get in the way of his telling her.

'Let's see if you can really be my assistant,' Ada said. 'You can record the book that Lisa has just borrowed. The one she returned, too. Let me show you how.'

What does she take me for? He suddenly felt furious. *Does she think I'm just a little child, that she'll let me play with her computer for a bit and then send me off to bed? How can she be such a dick-head? Doesn't she understand anything? Anything at all?* He felt a blind compulsion to hurt her, to bite her, crush her, pull off her big wooden

212

earrings, to make her wake up and understand at last.

She sensed she had made a mistake. Laying a hand on his shoulder she said:

'That's enough, Kobi.'

The touch of her hand on his shoulder made him dizzy, but it also made him sad, because he knew she was only trying to comfort him. He turned and, taking hold of her cheeks with both his hands under her earrings, he pulled her face round hard. Not daring to move his lips closer to hers he simply stayed holding her for a long time, with her cheeks between his hands and his eyes fixed on her lips, which were not open but not quite closed either. There was an expression he did not recognise on her face under the harsh neon light: she didn't look hurt or offended, he thought, but sad. He held her head gently but firmly, with his lips close to hers and his whole body trembling with desire and fear. She did not resist him or try to break free from his grasp but waited. At last she spoke:

'Kobi. We'd better be going.'

He let go of her face, and without taking his eyes off her he sprang up and felt for the light switch

213

with quivering fingers. In an instant the neon light went out and darkness filled the library. *Now*, he said to himself. *If you don't tell her now you'll regret it for the whole of your life. For ever.* As well as the conflicting desire and emotion he felt a vague urge to shelter and protect her. From himself.

5

HIS OUTSTRETCHED arms felt for her and found her where she stood motionless behind the desk. He held her in the darkness, not face to face but with his face against the side of her and his hips pressed against her waist, in a T shape. The darkness lent him courage and he kissed her ear and her temple, but he didn't dare to turn her towards him and seek her lips with his. She stood with her arms and hands hanging down at her sides, neither resisting him nor joining in. Her thoughts wandered to the stillborn child, born at five months after complications. The doctor had told her she could never have another child. During the gloomy months that followed she had blamed her husband for the baby's death, without any justification, except perhaps that he had slept with her on one of the nights before the stillbirth. She had not wanted him to but had let him have his way because ever since she was a child she had generally yielded before anyone with strong will power, especially if it was a man, not because she was naturally submissive, but because strong male will power gave her a feeling of safety and trust, together with acceptance and a desire to give in. Now she accepted the boy's sideways embrace without encouraging him or stopping him. She stood motionless, her arms dangling and her head hanging. But she sighed faintly, which Kobi could not interpret.

Was it a groan of pleasure such as he had heard in films, or was it a faint protest? But the powerful desire of an imaginative and sexually frustrated seventeen-year-old youth made him rub himself against her hip. And because he was a full head taller than she was, he drew her head to his chest and his lips gently hovered over her hair and lightly touched one of her earrings as though trying to distract her from what his loins were doing to her. His desire was not curbed by shame but if anything intensified: he knew that now he was destroying, trampling underfoot for ever, whatever might have developed between him and his beloved. This destruction made his head swirl, and his hand felt for her breast but he panicked and put his arm round her shoulders instead, while his loins went on rubbing against her hip until his spine and his knees were so flooded and shaken with pleasure that he had to hold onto her so as not to fall over. Feeling a wetness on his abdomen he hurriedly pulled away, not to soil her too. He stood panting and shaking in the darkness, very close to her but not touching her, his face burning and his teeth chattering. Ada broke the silence by saying gently:

'I'm turning the light on.'

'Yes,' said Kobi.

But she was in no hurry to turn on the light. She said:

'You can go over there and tidy yourself up.'

'Yes,' said Kobi.

Suddenly he murmured in the darkness:

'I'm sorry.'

He felt for her hand and held it and, nuzzling her with his lips, he apologised again, and felt his way

216

to the door and fled from the thick darkness in the library into the luminous darkness of the summer night. A half moon had risen above the water tower and was spreading a pale half-light over the rooftops, the treetops, and the shadowy hills to the east.

She switched on the dazzling neon light, and straightened her blouse with one hand and her hair with the other. She thought for a moment that he had just gone to the toilet, but the door of the library was wide open and she followed him out and stood on the doorstep, filling her lungs with the sharp night air that smelt vaguely of mown grass, cowpats, and some sweet flower she could not put a name to. *Why did you run away*, she said to herself, *why did you go, child, why were you so startled?*

She returned to the library, shut down the computer, switched off the air conditioning and the dazzling neon lights, then locked up and went home. She was accompanied by the singing of the frogs and the crickets and by a gentle breeze that carried a smell of thistles and dust. Maybe that child was lying in wait for her again behind some tree, maybe he would offer to walk her home again, maybe this time he would have the courage to hold her hand or put his arm round her waist. She felt that his smell, a smell of black bread, soap and sweat, was accompanying her. She knew that he would not come back to her, either this evening or probably on any of the following evenings. She felt sorry for his lone-liness, his regret and his pointless shame. Yet she also felt some kind of inner joy and spiritual exalt-ation, almost pride, that she had let him get carried away. How little he had wanted from her. And if he had wanted more she might not have stopped him. She took a deep breath. She was sad she had not said the simple words, 'Never mind, Kobi, don't be scared, you're fine, everything's fine now.'

The diesel tanker was not waiting for her outside her house, and she knew she would be alone tonight. At home she was greeted by two hungry cats that got under her feet and rubbed themselves against her legs. She spoke to them aloud, scolded them, lavished affection on them, gave them food and put water in their drinking bowls. Then she went to the toilet, and washed her face and neck and combed her hair. She switched on the TV in the middle of a programme about the melting of the polar ice cap and the destruction of the Arctic ecosystem. She buttered a slice of bread, spread cream cheese on it, sliced a tomato, cooked an omelette and then made herself a cup of tea. Then she settled in the armchair in front of the destruction of the Arctic ecosystem on the TV, sipped her tea, and hardly noticed that her cheeks were covered in tears. Even when she did become aware of it, she went on eating and drinking and staring at the TV, and merely wiped her cheeks a few times. The tears did not stop but she felt better, and she said to herself the words she had meant to say to Kobi: 'Never mind, don't be scared, you're fine, everything's fine now.' She got up, still in tears, picked up one of the cats and sat down again. At a quarter to eleven she stood up, closed the shutters, and switched off most of the lights.

6

KOBI EZRA wandered around the streets of the village. Twice he passed the Village Hall and the grocer's shop from which his family made a living. He entered the Memorial Garden and sat down on a bench that was already damp with dew. He wondered what she thought of him now and why she hadn't slapped his cheeks as he deserved. Suddenly he waved his arm and slapped his own face so hard that his teeth hurt, his ears rang and his left eye was bloodshot. Shame filled his body like some revolting viscous matter.

Two boys of his own age, Elad and Shahar, passed his bench without noticing him. He curled up and hid his head between his knees. 'They soon saw she was lying,' Shahar was saying. 'Nobody believed her for a second.' 'But it was a white lie,' Elad replied; 'I mean it was a justifiable lie.' They moved on, their shoes crunching on the gravel. What he had done tonight would never be wiped out, Kobi thought. Even when many years had passed and his life had taken him to places that he could not imagine. Even if he went to the big city to look for a prostitute, as he had often imagined doing. Nothing would eradicate the shame of what he had done tonight. He could have gone on chatting with her in the library and not turned out the lights. And even if he had lost his senses and turned out the lights, he could have used the cover of darkness to

220

express his feelings. Everybody said that words were his strong point. He could have used words. He could have quoted some lines from a love poem by Bialik or Yehuda Amichai. He could have confessed that he wrote poems himself. He could have recited one that he had written about her. On the other hand, he thought, she was also partly to blame, because she had behaved towards him the whole evening like an older woman with a child or a teacher with a pupil. She pretended I wait for her opposite the post office and walk her to the library just like that, for no particular reason. The fact is that she knew the truth and just pretended so as to spare my feelings. If only she hadn't, if only she had asked me about my feelings, however embarrassing it might be. If only I had had the guts to tell her to her face that someone like her had no reason to go running after tanker drivers. *You and I are twin souls and you know it. I can't help it if I was born fifteen years after you. Everything is lost now, after what happened. Lost for ever. And in fact what I did changed nothing, because it was doomed from the start. We never had a chance, either of us. There was never a shadow of hope. Maybe* (he thought)

*when I've finished with the army I'll get myself a
licence to drive a diesel tanker.*

He got up from the bench and walked across the
Memorial Garden. The gravel path crunched under
his sandals. A night bird made a ragged sound, and
far away at the edge of the village a dog barked
insistently. He had eaten nothing since lunchtime,
and he felt hungry and thirsty, but the thought of
the house where his parents and his sisters were
probably glued to the blaring television put him off.
True, if he went home nobody would say anything
to him or ask him anything; he could grab something to eat from the refrigerator and shut himself
up in his room. But what would he do in his room,
with his abandoned aquarium where a dead fish
had been floating for a week, and his stained mattress?
Better to stay out and maybe spend the whole night
roaming the empty streets. Maybe the best thing
would be to go back to that bench and lie down
on it, and sleep dreamlessly till morning.

Suddenly he got the idea of going to her house:
if the diesel tanker was parked outside he would
climb onto it and throw a lighted match inside so
everything would explode, for ever. He felt in his

222

pockets for matches, but he knew he didn't have any. Then his feet took him to the water tower that stood on its three concrete legs. He decided to climb the tower so as to be closer to the half moon that was floating now over the eastern hills. The rungs of the iron ladder were cold and damp; he climbed quickly and soon found himself at the top of the tower. Here there was an old concrete lookout post from the War of Independence, with broken sandbags and loopholes. He went inside and looked out through one of the holes. The place smelt of stale urine. The night stretched out before him in a wide, empty expanse. The sky was bright and the stars sparkled, strangers to each other and to themselves. From the depth of the darkness two shots rang out in swift succession. From here they sounded hollow. There were still lights on in the windows of the houses. Here and there he could see the bluish flicker of a TV screen through an open window. Two cars passed beneath him along Vine Street, their headlights illuminating for a moment the avenue of dark cypresses. Kobi looked for the windows of her house, and because he couldn't be sure he chose to concentrate on one which was more or less in the right

223

direction and decided that it was hers. A yellow light was shining there, through the drawn curtain. From now on, he knew, he and she would pass each other in the street like two strangers. He would never dare say a single word to her. She would probably avoid him too. If some day he had to go to the post office for something, she would look up from the counter behind the grille and say in a flat tone of voice:

'Yes? What can I do for you?'

224

Singing

1

THE FRONT door was open and cold, damp, winter air blew into the hall. When I arrived, between twenty and twenty-five people were already there, some of whom were still clustering in the hallway, helping each other off with their coats. I was greeted by a buzz of conversation and a smell of burning logs, wet wool and hot food. Almoslino, a big man wearing glasses attached by a cord, was bending over Dr Gili Steiner and kissing her on both cheeks. Slipping his hand round her waist he said:

'You're looking really splendid tonight, Gili.'

'Look who's talking,' she replied.

Plump Kormann, who had one shoulder higher than the other, gave Gili Steiner a big hug, then he hugged Almoslino and me, too.

'It's good to see you all,' he said. 'Did you see how it's raining out there?'

By the coathooks I bumped into Edna and Yoel

Rieback, a pair of dentists in their mid-fifties who had grown so alike over the years they seemed like twins; they both had short, grey hair, wrinkled necks and pursed lips. Edna Rieback was saying:

'Some people won't come today because of the rain. We nearly stayed at home ourselves.'

Her husband Yoel added: 'What is there to do at home? The winter dampens your soul.'

It was a wintry Friday evening in the village of Tel Ilan. The tall cypresses were shrouded in mist. Visitors were gathering at Dalia and Avraham Levin's for an evening of communal singing. Their home stood on a hill in a little lane called Pumphouse Rise. It had a tiled roof and a chimney, two storeys and a cellar. In the garden, which was lit by electric lights, stood some soggy fruit trees, olives and almond trees. In front of the house was a lawn bordered with beds of cyclamen. There was also a little rockery from which an artificial waterfall gurgled into an ornamental pond, where some lethargic goldfish swam to and fro lit by a light fixed in the bottom of the pool. The rain ruffled the surface of the water.

I left my coat on top of a heap of outdoor clothes on a sofa in a side room and made my way into the living room. Every few weeks about thirty people, mostly over fifty, gathered at the Levins'. Every couple brought a quiche or a salad or a hot dish, and they sat in the spacious living room filling the air with old Hebrew and Russian songs that had a melancholy, sentimental air. Yohai Blum would accompany the singing on his accordion while three middle-aged women sat around him playing recorders.

Above the hubbub that filled the room rose the voice of Gili Steiner, the doctor, who announced:

'Sit down everybody, please, we want to begin.'

But the guests were in no hurry to sit down; they were busy chatting, laughing and slapping each other on the shoulder. Tall, bearded Yossi Sasson cornered me by the bookcase.

'How are you, what's up, what's new?'

'No news,' I said, 'how about you?'

'Same as usual,' he replied, adding: 'Not great.'

'Where's Etty?' I asked.

'That's it,' he said. 'She's not too good. The thing is, they found some kind of nasty tumour this week. But she doesn't want anyone to talk about it. And apart from that . . .' He stopped.

'Apart from that what?'

But he said, 'Nothing. It's not important. Did you *see* how it's raining? Real winter weather.'

Dalia went round the room and handed each of her guests a photocopied songbook. Her husband Avraham had his back to the room: he was putting more wood on the wood-burning stove. Many years ago Avraham Levin was my commanding officer in the army. His wife, Dalia, studied history with me at the Hebrew University in Jerusalem. Avraham was a withdrawn, silent man, while Dalia was the gushing type. I was friends with each of them separately before they even knew one other. Our friendship continued after they married. It was a quiet, steady friendship that did not need constant proof of affection, nor did it depend on how often we met. Sometimes a year or more would go by between meetings, yet they still greeted me warmly. But for some reason I had never stayed the night in their house.

Some twenty years ago Dalia and Avraham had an only son, Yaniv. He was a somewhat solitary child, and as he grew older he became the kind of teenager who is always shut up in his room. When he was little, and I came to visit, he liked to press his head against my stomach and he would make himself a little lair under my pullover. Once I brought him a tortoise as a present. Four years ago, when he was sixteen, or so, the boy went into his parents' bedroom, crawled under their bed and blew his brains out with his father's pistol. They searched for him all over the village for a day and a half, not realising that he was lying under his parents' bed. Dalia and Avraham even slept in the bed without realising that their son's body was right underneath them. Next day when the cleaner came in to do the room she found him there, curled up as if he were asleep. He did not leave a note, so various theories circulated among their friends. Some said one thing, others another. Dalia and Avraham set up a small scholarship fund for students of singing, because Yaniv had sometimes sung in the village choir.

2

A YEAR or two after the boy's death Dalia Levin became interested in Far Eastern spirituality. She was head of the village library council, and it was on her initiative that a meditation group was started there. Every six weeks she had a community singing evening in her home. I used to attend these evenings occasionally, and because they accepted that I was a confirmed bachelor everyone greeted the various girl-friends I sometimes brought with me warmly. This evening I had come on my own, with a bottle of merlot for my hosts and the intention of sitting in my usual place, between the bookcase and the aquarium.

Dalia threw herself into those evenings in her home: she organised, phoned around, invited, greeted, seated, directed the singing from the songbooks that she had photocopied herself. Ever since the tragedy, she had given herself over to frenetic activity. Besides the library council and the meditation and the musical evenings she had all kinds of committees and councils, yoga classes, study days, conferences, work-shops, meetings, lectures, courses and excursions.

As for Avraham Levin, he became quite reclusive. Every morning at six-thirty precisely he started his car and drove to work at the Aerospace Research Centre where he specialised in the development of various systems. After work, at five-thirty or six, he came straight home. In summer he changed into a singlet and shorts and worked in the garden for an hour or so. Then he showered, had a light supper on his own, fed the cat and the goldfish, and settled down to read while listening to music and waiting for his wife to come home. He generally preferred baroque music, but sometimes he listened to Fauré or Debussy, or to jazz of the introspective variety.

In winter, when it was dark by the time he got home, he would lie down fully dressed on the rug next to the sofa in the living room, listening to music and waiting for Dalia to come home from her meeting or class. At ten o'clock he always went up to his room. They had abandoned their shared bedroom after the tragedy, and now slept in separate rooms at opposite ends of the house. No one went into the old bedroom: its shutters were permanently closed.

On Saturdays, summer and winter alike, Avraham went for a long walk shortly before sunset. He skirted the village from the south, crossing fields and orchards, and re-entered it from the north. He would go briskly past the water tower on its three concrete legs, walk the whole length of Founders' Street, turn left into Synagogue Street, cross the Pioneers' Garden, cross Tribes of Israel Street, and return home along Pumphouse Rise. If he passed anyone he knew, he would nod a greeting without stopping or even slowing. Sometimes he did not even acknowledge the passer-by, but kept on walking in a straight line, too deep in thought to notice.

3

As I was sitting down in my usual corner, between the aquarium and the bookcase, somebody called my name. I looked around but could not see who it was. On my right sat a woman in her fifties with her hair tied back in a little bun. I didn't know her. Opposite me there was just the window, with the darkness and rain beyond. To my left the tropical fish swam behind the glass of the aquarium. Who could have called me? Maybe I had imagined it. Meanwhile the sounds of conversation had died down and Dalia Levin was making announcements about the evening's programme. There would be an interval at ten o'clock, when a buffet supper would be served. Wine and cheese would be served at midnight precisely. She also announced the dates of the next meetings of the group.

I turned to the woman sitting next to me and

introduced myself in a whisper, asking if she played an instrument. She whispered that her name was Dafna Katz and said that she used to play the recorder but had given it up long ago. She said no more. She was tall and very thin, with glasses, and her hands seemed long and thin too. Her hair was gathered back in an old-fashioned-looking bun.

Meanwhile the whole group had begun to sing Sabbath Eve songs: 'The sun on the treetops no longer is seen', 'On Ginosar Valley the Sabbath comes down', 'Peace be with you, angels of peace'. As I joined in, a pleasant warmth spread through my body as though I had been drinking wine. I looked round the room, trying to work out who had called my name earlier, but everyone was busy singing. Some sang shrilly, others deeply, and some had a beatific smile on their lips. Dalia Levin, the hostess, held her body with her arms as if hugging herself. Yohai Blum began to play his accordion and the three women accompanied him on the recorder. One of them let out a loud discordant note, but she quickly corrected herself and played on in tune.

After the Sabbath songs, it was time for four or five pioneer songs about the Galilee and Kinneret, followed by some songs about winter and rain, since the rain was still beating on the windows and occasional rolls of thunder shook the panes, and the lights stuttered because of the storm.

Avraham Levin sat, as usual, on a stool by the door leading to the kitchen. He was not confident of his voice, so he did not join in the singing but sat listening with his eyes closed, as though it were his task to pick up any wrong note. From time to time he tiptoed out to the kitchen to check on the soups and quiches that were keeping warm for the buffet supper to be served in the interval. Then he would check the stove and sit down again, with bowed head, on his stool, and close his eyes once more.

4

THEN DALIA silenced us all. 'Now,' she said, 'Almoslino will sing us a solo.' Almoslino, the big heavy man with his glasses on a black cord round his neck, got to his feet and sang 'Laugh, oh laugh at all my dreams'. He was endowed with a deep, warm bass voice, and when he got to the line

'Never have I lost faith in people' it sounded as though he were in pain, speaking to us from the depths of his soul and expressing through the words of the song some new, heart-wrenching thought that none of us had ever heard before.

As the applause died down, Edna and Yoel Rieback stood up, this pair of dentists who looked like twins, with their short grey hair, their pursed lips and the ironic lines that had become etched round their mouths. They sang a duet, 'Spread your wings, O evening', and as they sang their voices intertwined like a pair of dancers clinging to one another. They followed this with 'Enfold me under your wing'. I reflected that if in this song Bialik, our national poet, asks what love is, who are we, those of us who are not poets, to boast of knowing the answer to this question? Edna and Yoel Rieback finished singing, bowed together to left and right, and we all applauded.

There was a short pause because Rachel Franco and Arieh Zelnik arrived late, and while they were taking off their coats they announced that, according to the news on the radio, Air Force planes had bombed enemy targets and returned safely to their base. Yohai Blum put his accordion down and said, 'At last.' Gili

Steiner answered him angrily that it was nothing to celebrate, violence only begot more violence and vengeance pursued vengeance. Yossi Sasson, the tall, bearded estate agent, said mockingly:

'So what are you suggesting, Gili? That we do nothing? Turn the other cheek?'

'A normal government,' Almoslino intervened in his deep bass voice, 'should act calmly and rationally in such situations, whereas ours, as usual, has a knee-jerk and superficial response . . .'

Just then Dalia Levin, our hostess, intervened and suggested that instead of arguing about politics we should get on with the singing, which was why we were all here.

Arieh Zelnik had removed his coat by now. He could not find a chair so he sat down on the rug at the Riebacks' feet, while Rachel Franco pulled up a stool she found near the coathooks in the hall and sat down just outside the open door, so as not to add to the crush in the room and because she had to leave in an hour to check on her old father whom she had left alone at home. I wanted to say something about the bombing raid, about which I had ambivalent views, but I was too late because the argument had died down and Yohai Blum was striking up on his accordion again. Dalia Levin suggested we continue with some love songs. She suited action to words, and launched into a song: 'Once upon a time there were two roses, two roses.' Everybody joined in.

At that instant I had a sudden feeling that I had to go at once to the room where I had left my coat on a pile of other coats and get something from one of the pockets. It seemed to be very urgent, but I couldn't remember what it was. Nor could I make out who it was who was apparently calling me again: the thin woman sitting next to me was still busy singing, while Avraham, on his stool by the kitchen door, had closed his eyes and was leaning against the wall, not joining in the singing.

My thoughts strayed to the empty streets of the village lashed by the rain, the dark cypresses swaying in the wind, the lights going out in the little houses, the drenched fields and bare orchards. I had the sensation at that moment that something was going on in some darkened yard and that it concerned me and I ought to be involved with it. But what it was I had no idea.

The group was now singing 'If you want me to

show you the city in grey', and Yohai Blum had stopped playing his accordion to make way for the three recorders that played in unison now and without any dissonance. Then we sang 'Where has your beloved gone, O most beautiful among women?' What was it that I had wanted to check so urgently in the pocket of my overcoat? I could not find an answer, so I suppressed the urge to go to the other room and I joined in the singing of 'The pomegranate wafts its scent' and 'My white-throated beloved'. In the interval before the next song I leant over and in a whisper I asked Dafna Katz, with the thin hands, who was sitting next to me, what these songs reminded her of. She seemed surprised by my question and answered, 'Nothing in particular.' Then she thought again and said: 'They remind me of all sorts of things.' I leant towards her again and was about to say something about memories, but Gili Steiner shot us a dirty look, as if to stop us whispering, so I gave up and went on singing. Dafna Katz had a pleasant alto voice. Dalia Levin was an alto, too. Rachel Franco was a soprano. And from across the room burst Almoslino's low, warm bass. Yohai Blum played his accordion and the three recorders wound round his playing like climbing plants. We felt good sitting in a circle on a rainy, stormy night singing old songs from the days when everything had seemed so clear and bright.

Avraham Levin got up wearily from his stool and put another log in the stove that warmed the room with a pleasant, gentle flame. Then he sat down again on the stool and closed his eyes, as though once more he had been given the task of spotting anyone who was singing out of tune. Outside, the rolls of thunder may have been rumbling on, or it may have been the Air Force planes flying low overhead on their way back from bombing enemy targets, but because of the singing and the music we could hardly hear them inside the room.

5

A T TEN o'clock Dalia Levin announced the break for the buffet and we all got up and started moving towards the corner of the room nearest the kitchen. Gili Steiner and Rachel Franco helped Dalia to get the pies and quiches out of the oven and to take the pots of soup off the stove, and many people crowded round the table and helped themselves to cups and paper plates. The conversations and arguments resumed. Somebody said that the council workers were right to strike and someone else replied that with all these justifiable strikes we would end up with the government printing more money again and we'd be back to the merry old days of galloping inflation. Yohai Blum, the accordionist, commented that it was wrong always to blame the government for everything – ordinary citizens must also share the blame, and he didn't exclude himself.

Almoslino was holding a bowl of steaming soup and eating standing up. The steam was misting up his glasses on their black cord. He declared that the press and the television always painted a gloomy picture. The general picture, he said, was much less dark than it was painted by the media. You would think, he added bitterly, that we were all thieves and all corrupt.

Almoslino's words seemed to carry authority because they were delivered in his resonant bass voice. Plump Kormann had heaped his plate with potato quiche, baked potato, a meatball and vegetables and was balancing it in one hand, and having trouble manoeuvring his knife and fork with the other. At that moment Gili Steiner offered him a glass of red wine. 'I haven't got enough hands,' he chuckled, so she stood on tiptoe and held the glass to his lips so that he could drink.

'Don't you think it's a bit too facile to blame the media for everything?' Yossi Sasson said to Almoslino.

'You have to see things in perspective,' I interposed, but Kormann, with one shoulder higher than the other, interrupted me and denounced one of the ministers in the government in outspoken terms.

'In any decent government,' Kormann said, 'someone like that would have had his marching orders long ago.'

'Just a moment, just a moment,' said Almoslino; 'maybe you could start by giving us your definition of a decent government.'

'Anyone would think all our problems started and ended with one person,' said Gili Steiner. 'If only they did. Yossi, you haven't tried the vegetable quiche. Why not?'

And Yossi Sasson, the estate agent, replied with a smile:

'Let me deal with what I've already got on my plate, and then I'll see where to go next.'

'You're all wrong,' said Dafna Katz, but what she was going to say was submerged in the general hubbub, with everyone talking at once and some people raising their voices. Inside everyone, I thought, there is the child they once were. In some you can see that it's still a living child; others carry around a dead child inside them.

I left the group in the middle of its argument and went over to talk to Avraham Levin, my plate in my hand. He was standing by the window, holding the curtain up and peering outside at the rain and the storm. I touched his shoulder lightly and he turned towards me without saying anything. He tried to smile, but merely managed to make his lips tremble.

'Avraham,' I said. 'Why are you standing here on your own?'

He thought for a moment, and then said:

'I find it difficult with so many people, all talking at once. It's hard to hear and hard to follow.'

'It's really winter out there,' I said.

'Yes, it is.'

I told him I'd come on my own because there were two women who had both wanted to come with me and I hadn't wanted to choose between them.

'Right,' Avraham said.

'Listen,' I said, 'Yossi Sasson told me in confidence that they've found some sort of a tumour in his wife. A nasty tumour, that's what he said.'

Avraham nodded a few times, as if agreeing with himself, or as if I had confirmed something that he had already guessed.

'If necessary, we'll help,' he said.

We pushed our way through the people who were standing eating from disposable plates, crossing the buzz of voices chatting and arguing, and went out onto the veranda. The air was cold and piercing and a fine drizzle was now falling. Lightning flickered indistinctly far away over the hills to the east, but there was no accompanying thunder. A deep, wide silence lay on the garden, on the fruit trees and the dark cypresses, on the lawn and on the fields and orchards that breathed in the darkness beyond the garden hedge. At our feet pale lights shone from the rocky bottom of the fishpond. A solitary jackal wailed in the depth of the darkness. And several angry dogs replied from the yards of the village.

'Look,' Avraham said.

I said nothing. I waited for him to tell me what

I should look at, what he was talking about. But Avraham fell silent. Finally I broke the silence:

'Do you remember, Avraham, when we were in the army, in seventy-nine, the raid on Deir an-Nashaf? When I got a bullet in my shoulder and you evacuated me?'

Avraham thought for a minute, and then said: 'Yes, I remember.'

I asked him if he ever thought about those days, and Avraham rested his hands on the cold, wet railing of the veranda and said, with his face to the darkness and his back to me:

'Look, it's like this, for a long time now I haven't thought about anything. At all. Just about the boy. I might have been able to save him, but I had a theory and I stuck to it, and Dalia followed me with her eyes closed. Let's go indoors. The break is over, they're starting to sing again.'

6

IN THE second half of the evening we started with some pioneer songs of the Palmach and songs from the War of Independence, like 'Dudu' and 'The Song of Friendship', and then we sang some songs by Naomi Shemer. Wait another hour and a half, announced Dalia, on the stroke of midnight we'll have another break and we'll serve wine and cheese. I sat in my place, between the bookcase and the aquarium, and Dafna Katz was sitting next to me again. She held onto her songbook with both hands, with all ten fingers, as though she were afraid that somebody might snatch it from her grasp. I leant over and asked her in a whisper where she lived, and if she had a lift home afterwards, because if not I'd be happy to take her. Dafna whispered that Gili Steiner had brought her and was going to take her home afterwards, thank you very much.

'Is this your first time here?' I asked.

Dafna whispered that it was her first time, but that from now on she was planning to make a point of coming every time, every six weeks.

Dalia Levin signalled to us, with a finger on her lips, that we should stop whispering. I took the songbook from Dafna's thin fingers and turned the page for her. We exchanged a swift smile and joined in the singing of 'In the night the wind is blowing'. Again I had the feeling that I ought to go and get something from the pocket of my overcoat on the heap of coats in the other room, but what it was I could not fathom. On the one hand I had a sense of panic, as though there were some urgent responsibility that I was ignoring, but on the other hand I knew the panic was false.

Dalia Levin signalled to Yohai Blum the accordionist and the three women who were accompanying him on the recorder, but they couldn't understand what she wanted. She stood up, went over to them, bent down and explained something, then she crossed the room and whispered to Almoslino, who shrugged his shoulders and seemed to refuse, but she insisted and pleaded, and finally he nodded. Then she spoke up, asked us all to be quiet for a moment, and announced that now we would sing a canon. We would sing 'Everything on this earth is transient', followed by 'I look up to the heavens and ask the stars above, Why does your light not reach me'. She asked her husband Avraham to dim the lights.

What was it that I had to check in the pocket of my overcoat? My wallet with my papers, I verified by touch, was with me in my trouser pocket. My driving glasses were in their case in my shirt pocket. Everything was here. Nevertheless as soon as the canon was over I got up, whispered an apology to my neighbour Dafna Katz, crossed the circle of guests, and went out into the passage. My feet took me into the hall and to the front door, which for some reason I opened a crack, but there was no one outside, only the drizzle. I retraced my steps along the passage as far as the door of the living room. Now everyone was singing some of Natan Yonatan's plaintive songs, such as 'Banks are sometimes yearning for a river', and 'Again the song is going forth, again our days are weeping'.

At the end of the passage I turned to a little side passage leading to the small room where I had left my overcoat in a pile of coats. I excavated for a while, pushing other people's coats away to left and right until I found my own. I checked the pockets slowly and methodically. In one there was a folded woollen scarf; in another I found some papers, a packet of sweets and a little torch. Because I didn't know what I was looking for, I went on searching in the inside pockets, where there were some more bits of paper and a pair of sunglasses in a case. I certainly didn't need sunglasses on this winter's night. So what was I looking for? I could find no answer, apart from a gnawing anger, at myself and at the heap of coats that I had scattered. I rebuilt the heap to the best of my ability and took the pocket torch with me as I turned to go. I meant to return to my place between the bookcase and the aquarium, next to bony Dafna Katz with her thin arms, but something stopped me. It may have been the fear that my entrance in the middle of a song would attract unwelcome attention, or it may have been a vague feeling that there was still something I ought to do in this house. But what it was I didn't know. I held onto the torch.

In the living room they were singing 'Would that I were a bird, a tiny little bird, eternally wandering, with a tormented soul'. The three recorders were playing without Yohai Blum's accordion. One of the recorders gave another little shriek but immediately corrected itself. Because I'd lost my place I went to the toilet, even though I didn't need to, but it was occupied, so I climbed upstairs, where there must be another one. From the top of the stairs the singing

250

sounded fainter, more wintry, so to speak, and even
though Yohai Blum's accordion had started up again
there seemed to be something muted about it. Now
everyone except me was singing a song by Rahel,
'Why did you lie to me, faraway lights', and I stood
on, enchanted and motionless, at the top of the
stairs.

7

I STOOD there for a few minutes, unable to decide
where I was headed. At the end of the upstairs
passage a single bulb gave out a weak light, just
enough to cast some shapeless shadows. A few
pictures were hanging on the walls of the passage,
but in the half-light they looked like vague grey
patches. Several doors opened off the passage, but
they were all closed. I went back and forth a couple
of times as though wondering which of them to try.
But I couldn't decide because I didn't know what I
was looking for and I had completely forgotten why
I had come upstairs. I could hear the wind outside.
The rain was stronger now and was beating on the

windows. Or it may have been hail. I stood in the passage for a while, considering the closed doors like a burglar wondering where the safe was hidden.

Then I cautiously opened the third door on the right. I was greeted by cold, distress and darkness. The air smelt as though the room had not been opened for a long time. I shone the torch inside, and saw shadows of furniture that swayed and merged as my hand holding the torch shook. The wind and the hail battered the closed shutters. The feeble light was reflected back at me from a large mirror on the door of the wardrobe, as though someone were trying to blind me. The stale odour in the room was a smell of dust and unchanged bedclothes. It was evidently a long time since anyone had opened a door or window here. There must be cobwebs in the corners of the ceiling, although I couldn't make them out. I could distinguish some pieces of furniture, a small chest of drawers, a chair, another chair. As I stood in the entrance I felt an urge to close the door behind me and lock it from the inside. My feet drew me inwards, into the depths of the room. The sound of singing downstairs was fainter now, no more than a soft murmur that was lost in the roar of the wind

252

and the clawing of the hail on the bedroom shutters. Outside, the garden must be wrapped in mist that blurred the outlines of the cypresses. There would be no living soul on Pumphouse Rise. Only the goldfish would be swimming, indifferent to the hail and the rain, in the pond that was lit from beneath by an electric beam. And the artificial waterfall would be trickling down the rockery and disturbing the surface of the water.

A big bed stood under the window, with a small bookcase on either side. There was a carpet on the floor and I took off my shoes and socks. The carpet was thick and deep, and felt soft and strange under my bare feet. I directed the beam of the torch at the bed and saw that it was covered with a bedspread on which were scattered some cushions. I had an impression that far away on the floor below me they were singing 'Can you hear my voice, my distant one?', but I could not be sure what my ears were hearing, or of what my eyes could see by the trembling light of the torch. There was a constant slow movement in the room, as if someone big and heavy were stirring sleepily in a corner, or crawling on all fours, or clumsily tumbling over and over, between the chest of drawers and the closed window. It must have been the quivering of the torch that produced this illusion, but I felt that behind my back, too, where the darkness was total, something was slowly creeping. I had no idea where from or where to.

What was I doing here? I had no answer to the question. And yet I knew that this abandoned bedroom was where I'd been wanting to come since the beginning of the evening and maybe for a long time before. I suddenly heard the sound of my own breathing and felt sorry that my breath punctured the damp silence that filled the room, since the rain had stopped, the wind had died down, and the singers downstairs had abruptly stopped singing. Maybe it was finally time for wine and cheese. I had no desire for wine or cheese. I had no further reason to turn my back on despair. So I got down on my hands and knees at the foot of the double bed and, rolling back the bedspread, I tried to grope with the pale beam of my torch into the dark space underneath.

In a faraway place at another time

ALL NIGHT long, poisonous vapours blow in from the green swamp. A sweetish smell of decay spreads among our huts. Iron tools rust here overnight, fences rot with a damp mould, mildew eats at the walls, straw and hay turn black with moisture, as though burnt in fire, mosquitoes swarm everywhere, our homes are full of flying and crawling insects. The very soil bubbles. Woodworm, moths and silverfish eat away the furniture, the wooden palings, and the wooden roofs. The children are sick all summer with boils, eczema and gangrene. The old folk die from atrophy of the airways. The stench of putrefaction comes even from the living. There are many people who are crippled, who suffer from goitre, from mental deficiency, twisted limbs, facial tics, drooling, because they all interbreed: brothers and sisters, sons and mothers, fathers and daughters.

I was sent here twenty or twenty-five years ago

by the Office for Underdeveloped Regions, and I
still go out every evening at twilight to spray the
swamp with disinfectant; I administer quinine,
carbolic acid, sulphur, skin ointments and antipara-
sitic drugs to the suspicious locals; and I encourage
a hygienic and abstinent lifestyle and distribute
chlorine and DDT. I'm holding the fort until a
replacement arrives, perhaps someone younger with
a stronger character than mine.

In the meantime I am the pharmacist, teacher,
notary, arbitrator, nurse, archivist, go-between and
mediator. They still doff their shabby caps to me
and clasp them to their chest as a mark of honour,
bow and scrape with sly, toothless smiles, and
address me in the third person. But increasingly I
have to curry favour with them, turn a blind eye,
accommodate their vain beliefs, ignore their impu-
dent grimaces, put up with their body odour and
bad breath, overlook the outrageous obscenity that
is spreading through the village. I have to admit to
myself that I have no power left. My authority is
dwindling. I only have left some tattered shreds of
influence that I exercise by means of subterfuges,
honeyed words, necessary lies, veiled threats and

little bribes. All that I have left to do is to hang on a little longer, until my replacement arrives. Then I shall leave this place for ever, or else I might take over an empty hut, get myself a lusty peasant wench, and settle down.

Before I came here, a quarter of a century ago or more, the district governor once came on a visit, surrounded by a large retinue. He stayed for an hour or two, and gave orders for the course of the river to be diverted so as to put an end to the malignant marsh. The governor was accompanied by officers and secretaries, surveyors, holy men, a legal expert, a singer, an official historian, one or two intellectuals, an astrologer, and representatives of the sixteen secret services. The governor dictated his orders: dig, divert, dry out, dig up, cleanse, inject, remove, upgrade, and turn over a new leaf.

Nothing has happened since.

Some say that over there, beyond the river, beyond the forests and mountains, a succession of governors has taken his place: one was ousted, one was defeated, another fell from grace, a fourth was assassinated, a fifth was imprisoned, a sixth turned his coat, a seventh fled or fell asleep. Here everything has remained as it always was: the old folk and babies continue to die and the young grow old before their time. The population of the village, if my cautious statistics can be trusted, is in terminal decline. According to the graph I have drawn up and hung over my bed, not a single person will be left alive here by mid-century. Just the insects and creepy-crawlies.

In fact, large numbers of children are born here, but most of them die in infancy and are hardly missed. The young men escape to the north. The girls grow beetroot and potatoes in the thick mud, they have their first child at twelve, and by twenty they seem worn out. Sometimes in an access of mad lust the whole village is swept up in a night of debauchery by the light of bonfires of damp wood. They all commit outrageous acts: old men with children, girls with cripples, humans with beasts. I cannot communicate the details as on such nights I barricade myself into the dispensary, where I live, and go to sleep with a loaded pistol under my pillow, in case they get any bright ideas.

But such nights occur infrequently. The next day

they wake at midday, heavy-headed, bleary-eyed, and go back to squelching submissively in their muddy fields from dawn to dusk. The days are ferociously hot. Insolent fleas, as big as a coin, swoop down on us and as they bite they emit a nauseous, piercing squeak. The work in the fields seems back-breaking. The beetroot and potatoes that are extracted from the spongy mud are nearly all rotten, yet they are eaten either raw or cooked in a foul, putrid liquid. The gravedigger's two elder sons ran away to the mountains and joined a gang of smugglers. Both their wives, with the children, moved into the hut of their younger brother, a boy of barely fourteen.

As for the gravedigger himself, a taciturn solidly built hunchback, he decided not to pass over this in silence. But the weeks and months went by in total silence, and the years went by. Then one day the gravedigger, too, moved in with his youngest son. More and more children were born there, and nobody knew which of them were the offspring of the runaway brothers, who sometimes spent a nocturnal hour or two in the village, and which were from the loins of the youngster, or indeed the

261

gravedigger or his elderly father. Whatever the truth, most of the babies died within a few weeks of being born. Other men came and went there at night, and simple-minded women, too, in search of a roof or a man, or shelter or a child or food. The present governor has not replied to the three urgent memoranda, each more serious than the last, sent at short intervals to warn of the deterioration of the moral climate and demand his immediate intervention. I was the outraged author of these memoranda.

The years pass in silence. My replacement has still not come. The policeman has been ousted in favour of his brother-in-law. Rumour has it that the original policeman has joined the smugglers in the mountains. I am still doing my duty, but I am becoming increasingly weary. They no longer address me in the third person, nor do they bother to doff their threadbare caps to me. There is no disinfectant left. The women are gradually emptying the dispensary of its drugs, without giving me anything in exchange. My intellect is waning along with my desires. I can no longer find enough light within myself. The thinking reed is becoming empty of thoughts. Or maybe it is my eyes that are becoming dimmed, so that even the midday light seems murky, and the queue of women waiting at the door of the dispensary looks like a row of sacks. Over the years I have become accustomed to their rotten teeth and their stinking breath. So I go on gently from morning to evening, from day to day, from summer to winter. I long ago stopped noticing the insect bites. My sleep is deep and peaceful. There is moss growing on my bedding and damp rot has invaded the walls. Some peasant woman or another takes pity on me from time to time and feeds me a gelatinous liquid made apparently from potato skins. All my books are going mouldy. The covers crumble away and fall off. I have nothing left, and I can barely distinguish between one day and the next, between spring and autumn, between one year and the next. Sometimes at night I seem to hear the distant wail of some primeval wind instrument: I have no idea what it is or who plays it, or whether it comes from the forest or the hills or from inside my skull, under my hair that is turning grey and thinning. So I am gradually turning my back on everything around me and, in fact, on myself as well.

Apart from one event that I witnessed this morning, which I shall report now in writing, without expressing an opinion.

This morning the sun rose and transformed the marshy vapour into a dense, viscous rain. Warm summer rain that smelt like an unwashed, sweaty old man. The villagers were beginning to come out of their huts and preparing to go down to the potato fields. Suddenly, on top of the hill to the east, a healthy, handsome man appeared, between us and the rising sun. He started waving his arms, describing all manner of circles and spirals in the damp air, kicking, bowing, jumping on the spot, without uttering a sound. 'Who is that man?' the village men asked one another. 'What is he looking for here?' 'He's not from here, and he's not from the next village, and he's not from the hills either,' the old men said. 'Perhaps he's come down from a cloud.'

'We must watch out for him,' said the women. 'We must catch him red-handed. We must kill him.'

While they were still discussing and arguing, the yellowish air filled with a rush of sounds, of birds, dogs, bees, mooing, scolding, buzzing of insects as big as beer mugs. The frogs in the swamp joined in and

264

the chickens were not slow to follow suit; harnesses jangled, there were coughs, groans and cursing. All sorts of different sounds.

'That man,' the gravedigger's young son said, and then he stopped.

'That man,' said the innkeeper, 'wants to seduce the girls.'

The girls shrieked: 'Look he's naked, look how big it is, look he's dancing, he's trying to fly, look, like wings, look, he's white right through to the bone.'

And the old gravedigger said: 'What's the good of all this chatter? The sun is up, the white man who was there, or who we imagined was there, has disappeared behind the bog. Words won't help. Another hot day is beginning and it's time to go to work. Whoever can work, let him work, put up, and shut up. And whoever can't work any more, let him die. And that's all there is to it.'